A Short Story of Love in Languedoc

Jack Victor

Publishing Push LTD

First paperback edition 2024

978-1-80541-451-3 (paperback)

978-1-80541-452-0 (ebook)

Contents

Chapter One

Paradise Found

Some believe an ageing Harry Potter look-a-like called Peter Mayle started the English invasion of the warming climes of the coastal regions of southern France, those shores that abut against the azure Mediterranean sea, when he expounded about neighbouring Provence. But any Anglo-French historian will tell you that the truth is that the great river valleys in the centre and much of the coast running down the Bay of Biscay once belonged, on and off, to English kings and queens, which is undoubtedly why there is still an endearing, if not strained, kinship between the French and English, and which still blends our languages and our very identities.

However, it is very apparent that the English cousins would rather exchange lives with their French counterparts than the other way around. Every year the French infrastructure booms with an excess of right-hand drive vehicles with the 'GB' sticker emblazoned on them. How many left hand drive cars do you see flooding onto the gridlocked English roads? Setting aside the Le Mans and Beaujolais expeditions, every year craggy faced Frenchmen sit outside bars on undulating French B roads and view the influx. It is a testament to the French disposition that they don't continually shake their heads in dismay. The secondary roads and the towns along their routes seem ageless. The new autoroute infrastructure attempts to woo and take most of the traffic in exchange for less time but many still prefer the free, meandering B roads. In comparison to the British roads they are still not busy though, which is completely understandable when you consider that France is almost twice the size of the UK but has a similar sized population.

It was down these, dappled, lime tree lined B roads, four years ago, that an ageing blue MGB roadster with shiny chrome bumpers glinting in the sunlight, had been driven by an even more ageing driver. Beside the driver a vivacious, much younger, blonde woman sat in the passenger seat. She was resting her hand on the driver's leg and letting the wind tousle the hair that had worked its way loose from the Hermes patterned silk scarf that covered her head. The large, round Chanel sunglasses she wore could not cover the fact she was a beautiful looking woman, who looked much younger than her 35 years.

The driver, Gerald, was in his late fifties and as skinny and fit as a greyhound. A grey greyhound, his full head of straight hair was now slightly receding but with his sharp features, it gave Gerald a distinguished air. One could deduce that his looks would have given him a depth of self-confidence; however, in contrast, he was by nature a quiet man who shied away from conflict and association with people. He had never married which may appear strange and unusual as, in his own way, he was, as described, quite a handsome man, if perhaps a little dull. As such, ever since his school days, he had been timid and uncomfortable around the fairer sex. The routine of living in his rented flat and travelling to and from his work continued this impact on his personal life and he hadn't even been in a lasting relationship of any kind. He had no family to speak of and was an only child; both his parents had separated earlier in his life and later died in other relationships. But on a positive note, this now meant that he was financially sound. The small amounts of inheritance he received from each of his parent's estates he had ploughed into separate pension schemes and with his own employment pension, for the moment, he could want for nothing as long as he remained reasonably frugal.

Gerald had initially been unaware of, and then overwhelmed by, the advances of the beautiful Annabelle only months prior to his advertised retirement. She had been temping for one of the pregnant administration ladies downstairs. He had barely noticed Annabel, the new girl in the office, looking at him intently and fluttering her eyelashes. Why would he? After all, why would a lovely young thing like Annabel be interested in a retiring old boy like Gerald? All that Gerald knew was that Annabel was always late, always took an hour for lunch instead of the customary forty five minutes, and was always first out of the door at the end of the day. She also did not appear to be very efficient at her job but the male supervisors and managers didn't appear to mind this at all. Gerald, eventually, egged on by many of his bullish male colleagues, had succumbed to Annabelle's very obvious advances.

Annabelle did not want to be at work; she did not want to work, full stop. She had recently fallen out with her father, Mark, over the reduction of her allowances and the 'heart to heart' conversation that her father had initiated at short notice. He had called her to his club in Pall Mall on the pretence that he wanted to have lunch with his life partner, Paul, and his only daughter. Annabelle, completely unsuspecting and looking forward to a night in London, accepted the offer without hesitation.

At the table overlooking the enclosed gardens at the rear of the Reform Club, Mark began,

"My darling, you know I love you so very much. We love you," he paused reaching out to hold Paul's hand. Paul gave an encouraging nod. Mark continued.

"Annabelle, you know, we just want the very best for you and to that end Paul has managed to find an opportunity at one of his friend's companies here in London. It's just temping at the moment but we're told the position will become permanent. It will be a great stepping stone into a business where you could make an independent and viable future."

Annabelle said nothing and continued to concentrate her gaze down and to nibble at her trout terrine. She took a sip of the chilled Chablis, her lipstick lightly fringing the glass rim. She placed the glass down and looked directly and only at her father.

"Daddy, you know I appreciate everything you do for me but I really don't believe I'm ready for such a commitment in my life at the moment. I have so much going on." She looked down and continued to eat her starter. Mark glanced quickly at Paul again with a visible wince.

"My darling," he continued "You're 35 years old. You have to start to make your own way. We cannot continue to support you financially and I know your mother certainly can't. You can continue to use the apartment but you have to find the money to pay the bills and support your own lifestyle. We'll still help you out with certain things but this has to happen Annabelle. You have to take this job!"

Since birth Annabelle had been the 'it' girl. Her parents had doted on her. Her parents, when married and together had ensured she had attended the finest schools. She had always been beautiful and lucky enough to be academically astute. At New Hall, her finishing school in Essex, she had been captain of the swimming and hockey teams and voted most likely to succeed in her final year book. Her parents fully expected her to continue to university and follow her father into the bank as a trader. It was just at this time her parents had split amicably and her father had set up a new home with Paul. Her whole world tipped upside down. Her mother moved to the family villa in Portugal and so she rested financially on her father. She didn't like Paul. She blamed him, in a very restricted view, for upsetting her world. By aged 25 most of her 'friends' had disowned her because of her father's preferred lifestyle. For the next ten years she found and honed a life skill, that, with her father's stipend, kept her financially where she wanted to be. Annabelle identified that older men, much older men, would pay handsomely to have her airy personality and beauty around them. At first she found it was the men at her father's golf club that she attracted. The men were stereotypically overweight and spending most of the week at the club away from their understanding but relieved wives; they were easy prey. She became expert in running and entertaining more than one benefactor. Emotions for Annabelle were a thing of the past; she likened herself to Blondie's 'Sunday Girl' lyric, 'cold as ice cream and twice as sweet'. The gifts rolled in and rolled back out to the pawn shop. Dinners out were never an issue, always free with a telephone call. The sex was easy and quick and only cemented her hatred for the situation that had got her to this place in life and actually, men in general.

Annabelle pushed her starter plate away from her; she finished her wine, dabbed her mouth with her crisp white napkin and stood up. She looked directly at her father again and said,

"Daddy, I appreciate your offer but I will have to decline. Keep your money!" She looked about the club's stately dining room as she said it. She continued, "you clearly need it more than your only daughter. I'll stay at the flat for as long as you can afford to keep me there. I'll expect the eviction notice sometime in the future." With that she grabbed her Hermes bag and looking back at just her father she said softly, "I hate you both for what you've done to me."

She walked off out of the dining room and tip-tapped slowly down the marble staircase to the foyer and out to Pall Mall, past the flaming torches at the entrance. She had to ready herself for her later meeting with a man who could have been taken for her grandfather. Mark's eyes had welled with tears as she left; Paul squeezed his hand.

Annabelle later took the job her father had offered. Once there, in Gerald she saw an opportunity.

To Gerald, it had been a whirlwind romance fuelled by the many champagne dinners in London that Annabelle loved so. At his retirement party, and after being plied with a substantial number of glasses of cheap prosecco, Gerald found himself being whisked away in the firm grip of Annabel at the end of the event. That evening Gerald was invincible with Annabel on his arm. Every bar door opened to them. Rules restaurant in Maiden Lane found a table that wasn't previously available and a box at the Palladium seemed, surprisingly, to be free. The following morning Gerald woke in a bijou room at the back of the Savoy Hotel with a heavy head and a substantially heavier credit card bill. But both those things filtered into the dull morning sky outside when he found the warm and sleepy Annabel under the covers next to him in the bed. Gerald worked the rest of the following week to finish his time but that week flew by as Annabel was with him every day and every evening. The following week when Gerald was at home, on his first week of retirement, Annabel had amazingly managed to get the week off work. It was whilst out at one of the frequent pub lunches that

Gerald had apparently had the brilliant idea to 'just get out and see some of Europe'. Annabel leapt up and claimed it an inspired thought. She enthused about 'living for living,' 'setting off into the sun' and 'dropping out for a simple life'. Gerald, who was normally staid in his ways looked into her blue, pleading eyes and said, "Why not!"

And as usual Gerald was rewarded later with a very short and clinical bout of passion.

Two months later, Gerald had given notice to the Singh family on his small, rented flat, disposed of all his unusable assets, bought the teal blue convertible MGB on eBay and they had left a cold, grey Hertfordshire for the Channel Tunnel. They had meandered down through France via Paris where Annabelle's favoured phrase tended to be 'You can't take it with you, Gerry' before purchasing ever more frivolous clothing and accessories. It had taken nearly three weeks for them to float southerly and rudderless, into the region of Languedoc-Roussillon. It was Annabelle who spotted Chateau Savinien glinting in the distance and cooed, "Ooh! Let's stop for a bite, Gerry!"

The town of Clairville is, frankly and *Frenchly,* generic in its look in that it could be many of the other towns that the pin-prick on a map of the region of Languedoc- Roussillon had identified. It is in one of the most fertile and glorious areas of southern France, producing some of the highest quantities of superb wines in the country. The region sits just below a line drawn between the light summery bodied regions of Midi Pyrenes and Provence, and it is a region that has all the benefits of the Cote D'Azur and Provence but none of the airs, graces or crowds. Clairville is a small town, set in the southern-most fringes of this diverse and cultural region, built on a large escarpment rising from the lush plains that circle it, the town sits like a large, white, chocolate cookie crumb discarded and melting on the patchwork quilt of fields surrounding it. Bright, white stone houses speckle the surrounding warm countryside. The main town sits on the top of the granite outcrop and is dominated by the Chateau Savinien. This is of small *castle* proportions, with glimmering, slate-topped spires rising to the skies from the towers which are grafted onto the rock at their base. The chateau perches precariously on the cliff, to one side of the formation. This gives the impression that the town could easily topple over onto its side if nudged, when approaching from the south. The chateau oversees an ordered *melange* of sunflowers, tall corn and manicured rows of vines, all set below a constant blue, Van Gogh sky.

On the plateau to the rear of the chateau the roads of the town radiate in Baron Haussman's Parisian fashion from the axis of the main square. The centre of the square has a large covered market; open on all sides, the pink tiled, orangery styled, roof is supported by a large number of cast iron pillars with intricate filigree buttresses propping the cross-members. On each side of the square, on the peripheral cobbled road, there are colour washed, three storey buildings with accommodation in the upper levels and small individual bars and restaurants cowering under their awnings that stretch out over the walkways. The independent traders, boulangeries, pharmacist and post office that dot the roads leading from the square provide the essentials for the town. Some of the shops on the side streets are such that they would never survive in the retail fast-lane of England; like the small electrical and house-wares shop selling everything from the crucial corkscrew, in varying disguises, to overpriced washing machines and refrigerators. The market, in days gone by, was a rendezvous point for every trader, grower and livestock owner in the area. Each town had its own market day in order not to conflict with the neighbouring towns. Now they contrive to serve the towns socially rather than in the support of insular livelihoods. The young people tend their city businesses rather than the fields now; trade has changed. One thing is constant though—the vines; the vines would never change, nor the production of the fabulous wines that flood the world. It is one of the rural trades that still provides some employment.

The wine was one of the parts of 'the dream' that latterly brought the influx of the Frenchman's cousins who craved the inexpensive properties left by the young French who no longer wanted them. Many have since written about what they came looking for and although a cliché, it was a dream: the slower life, the appreciation of every minute, the peace, the lack of light pollution, the warmth of the people similar to the weather, the uncrowded land and of course the food and wine. The invasion had surely been slower than the Nazis in 1940 but it had been steady nonetheless, and in all probability been going on since the 12th Century. Now the British *ex-pats* pervaded the rolling topography. You could surmise that they cut a standard profile; you could be collective, as the English are about the Frenchman wearing a beret and striped jumper, riding a bike with a string of onions around their neck. But, as we know, reality often bears a different image. Typically these English men and women are, for the most part, moneyed in some form. They are able to purchase a property and 'do it up'. They are able to survive by setting up in business, or are on pensions that enable them to live handsomely in this idyllic land, getting by, speaking *Franglais*. The seasons and the diet are kinder to them and therefore ensures longevity for their ageing bodies.

But back to Clairville; the main proportion of the population is still Gallic but they now welcome the English contingent. They understand their importance in bringing the new trade that their children were uninterested in, and that kept them alive – tourism. The visitor's new small fruit businesses, photographic studios, fruit growing, wine and gite accommodation ensured, in season, that their money would prop up the local economy. Sunflower seeds, wine and dusty chateaus will bring in some trade but the new immigrant townsfolk also give business to the local tradesmen and *immobilier*. The French and the English in Clairville mix like long lost friends in the main. But there will always be that cultural divide; the English are always unsure what their contemplative hosts think of them; but really they don't care anyway. After all they also have their characters, individual idiosyncrasies, moods and motives. This is what makes the melting pot in this little piece of paradise so interesting.

When Gerald and Annabel arrived in Clairville all that time ago, the town did what it did so well to many before—it drew them in and hugged them with an all-enveloping embrace that made it feel like home. That first week the happy couple stayed at the Hotel De Ville, exploring the local countryside, enjoying the warm evenings at the twice weekly night market, or outside the little restaurant across from the hotel. They browsed the local immobilier and dreamed of what could be. They even got the town's only estate agent, Philip Renoir, to show them some of the wonderful properties that not only were for sale, but also out of the price of Gerald's dwindling commutation cash. It was on one such excursion that Annabel noticed a small card in the immobilier window for an apartment for rent, two roads back from the market square. Gerald didn't take much persuasion; after all it was cheaper to rent than staying at the hotel. It was a sunny afternoon in May when the couple were led to Madame Joella's vast town house by the super friendly agent. With a little reduction in the rent, after some negotiation, Gerald and Annabel had collected their possessions from the hotel and were moved in by 7pm with a month's rent paid in advance.

Gerald loved Annabel, and Gerald loved Clairville. He loved the fact they were living together in their cosy top floor apartment. In truth he was still bemused that she loved being with him but he honestly believed that it was his faithfulness and his ability to make her laugh when they were out dining most days. Gerald did try a foray to the local *supermarche* on a number of occasions in an effort to impress Annabel with his culinary skills, but when he did, she would just laugh and inevitably they would go out to eat. This wasn't a problem to Gerald as he understood his cooking wasn't up to much. He just wanted the happy times to continue; however Gerald couldn't help but get the slight concern over his dwindling finances from his head. Then he would think with a sigh, in the manner of Annabelle, 'money doesn't buy you happiness'.

In an effort to stem this depreciation, Gerald managed to sell his beloved MG to a vehicle trader in the next town and bought from the same trader, what he thought was a quaint and very French, grey Renault 4, which he named Bella. He proudly drove back to Clairville and went to fetch Annabel from her nap at the apartment. He led her to where he had parked Bella. Gerald covered the excited Annabel's eyes and unleashed his surprise purchase.

"Annabelle, meet Bella!" Annabelle stared in amazement at the little grey French car with its bulbous roof and sliding windows.

"Where's the MG, Gerald?" she asked, even though she knew the awful truth already. Gerald noticed that Annabelle had reverted to Gerald from 'Gerry'. That couldn't be good, he thought.

"Oh, Annabelle, don't you think she's cute? She's economical, and got better vision for the lanes around here. And she's French!" Annabelle continued to stare at the dull grey car. "I got her for a third of the price of the MG, so that will help with the old finances," Gerald said, and immediately regretted saying it.

Annabelle turned slowly and purposefully to Gerald. She half whispered,

"Gerald, how do you expect me to be seen arriving at the golf course or Chez Michel in this!" She thought, and continued, "In fact, Gerald, this is truly a false economy when we will now have to arrange for a taxi every time we want to eat out or, in fact, go anywhere with a touch of class." Annabelle turned on her heel and began to walk the route back to the apartment.

"But Annabelle..." Gerald's wavering tone blurted. Annabelle did not break her heeled stride but simply held up the back of her flat hand above her shoulder to Gerald. Gerald sighed and turned to Bella. "Sorry old girl; I'm sure she'll come around to you eventually," he said quietly.

Gerald had broached the subject of finances with Annabel at least twice before. On both occasions Annabel had explained that she found financial matters so boring and in some respects, depressing. Gerald hadn't broached the subject again and eventually Annabelle had reluctantly begun driving Bella, constantly cursing the ridiculous gear changes.

Gerald extended his efforts to support the slowly reducing cash account by taking a labouring job at the nearby vineyard, just outside the town. It was called Domaine Saint-Patrice; they paid cash and he got a plastic, two-litre milk bottle filled with the cheaper wine of his choice for every day that he worked. Things were looking brighter and Gerald felt happier and more confident that he was providing. Even Annabel seemed brighter and happier in the latter summer months.

Gerald thought that it probably helped that she was getting some exercise now that she had taken up tennis at the local golf club. Gerald listened intently to Annabel as she expounded how she was, in her coach Gianni's words, 'extending her forearm swing well' and 'perfecting her serve'. An unfortunate side effect of the tennis was the fact Gianni, apparently, only took cash payments for his coaching. So Gerald would return in Bella from the vineyard, hand half his day's money to Annabel and she would drive off in Bella to the golf club for her lessons. Usually Annabel wouldn't get back until later in the evening and Gerald would have eaten his share of what he had prepared, and finished half of the milk carton of wine. Annabel, strangely, never seemed to be hungry when she came back from her lessons.

It was a sunny Thursday in mid-September at about 3pm, as Gerald remembered, that he came back to the apartment. He had finished early at the vineyard because he had booked a surprise meal at Annabel's favourite restaurant, Chez Michel, for the anniversary of when he and Annabel had crossed the Channel together to start their new lives. Gerald had worried lately that they were falling into a routine that left Annabel laughing less and less. Gerald walked in to the apartment and saw Annabel dressed in her favourite, short summer dress. Her make-up and hair were perfect. She was standing beside a newly packed pull-along Louis Vuitton suitcase. Gerald noticed some of the drawers in the chest open and emptied. He stood for a second looking at an equally stunned Annabel. She composed herself in an instant.

"Gerald, I was going to talk to you about this but I've been finding it very hard to get through to you."

A full five seconds passed and Gerald was still unable to move, then he said with a nervous smile.

"I've booked us a meal at Chez Michel; shall we go and talk about it there?"

"It's no good, Gerry...I need some time, some space. I feel as if I'm being restricted. I do love you, you know I do, but I need to find out a bit more about myself."

With this Annabel briefly looked at the red enamel Cartier watch Gerald had bought her in Paris, grabbed the handle to her case and breezed past him in the doorway, her Chanel perfume leaving a trail in her wake. Gerald intuitively followed her perfume trail down the large stone stairs as she clunk, clunk, clunked her way down them with the suitcase.

He said, "Annabel, please, can we talk? At least let me carry your case. Can I take you somewhere in the car?"

Annabel half laughed but composed herself again and replied,

"Gerry, please, you're making this more difficult than it has to be. Please give me some space." She flashed him a half smile and said, "look, just go back to the apartment and I'll give you a call tomorrow."

Gerald continued to follow Annabel as she wheeled her way to the market square where she half ran across the covered square and Gerald noticed her demeanour change as she flashed a smile and a wave to a dark haired, tanned man standing beside a gleaming red Alfa Romeo Spyder. Gerald stopped in his tracks, his vineyard dungarees hanging as loosely as his soul on his sloping shoulders. Annabel ran to the car and kissed the man on the cheek. She left the case and walked back to where Gerald was standing with his mouth half open. The tanned man loaded the case into the open rear seat of the Alfa Romeo. Annabel stopped a few feet from Gerald.

"Gerry, it's nothing really my darling; I told you I needed to find myself, to have some time without boundaries. Gianni mentioned he was going to drive back to Umbria to see his family, so I thought it would be an ideal time for you and I to take a break. I'll call you when I've had a few days to get my mind sorted. It'll all be alright darling."

With that Annabel turned on her fine heels and tip-toed across the cobbles to the open passenger door of the awaiting Alfa Romeo and Gianni. The rasping exhaust note of the Alfa Romeo reverberated around the market place, echoing off the tightly packed houses as it moved swiftly off and weaved out of the square towards the main road to the autoroute. Gerald saw Annabel look back with a wide smile and she raised her hand to wave to him and placed her other hand on Gianni's shoulder.

How long Gerald stood there after the sound of the exhaust died he didn't remember. He walked back across the cobbled square and wandered, in a daze, up Rue Garibaldi to where he found the open door of the local bar, Le Petit Lemon. A warm waft of cigar smoke and the mixed bouquet of coffee and pastis whirled around him. The aroma was warm and strong and in some way comforting but couldn't cut through his despair; it drew him, dream-like, inside the bar. Gerald had never been inside before as Annabel always thought it a common place and full of awful, leering, Frenchmen. Gerald walked inside and sat at the large, deep mahogany bar on a heavy cast stool with a thickly padded suede top seat, in the same colour as the bar. He placed the plastic milk carton full of rosé wine that he hadn't let go of, or in fact noticed, since he had returned earlier from the vineyard, on to the bar. Behind it, the bar owner, Hugo, said nothing. He had seen his fair share of men with problems, stresses or a breaking heart, walk into his treasured bar. He reached forward and lifted the plastic bottle of rosé from the bar, unscrewed the green top and sniffed the escaping vapour. He raised his bushy left eyebrow and dropped the corners of his mouth under his full beard in appreciation. He took down a large glass from the back of the bar and dropping a sizeable chunk of ice into it with a 'clink' filled it with some of the rosé'. He placed this in front of Gerald, whose gaze had not lifted from the shining bar. Hugo poured himself a smaller glass of the same rosé to savour before putting the uncomplicated container in the wine cooler. Nothing was said. Gerald did not leave Le Petit Lemon until the early hours of the following morning.

Chapter Two

Le Petit Lemon

In the town at the north end of the market place there's a large, double road width, cobbled area where some of the smaller, covered stalls are pitched on market days. This is both a vehicular and pedestrian area. In the corners of the market place the side streets lead out to the other parts of the town. Looking out from the covered market to this wide cobbled area one can see Rue Garibaldi leading out on the left. It goes straight up to the centrally placed town square. It is only a short length, some 45 metres, and the end of this road can clearly be seen as it opens onto the town square with its dappled trees and monument to the war dead centrally placed. It is the wider of the two northerly radiating roads, with a footpath on both sides. At the end of Rue Garibaldi on the left hand corner as you enter the square, sits a bar, Le Petit Lemon. The bar occupies the whole of the corner of Rue Garibaldi and the square. On the Rue Garibaldi's flank there are two large bi-fold, half glazed, hardwood doors. These are framed either side by large piers which are clad from floor to lintel height in lustrous, glossy, bottle green, ceramic tiles. The corner pier wraps around to the much wider front of the bar facing out onto the square where a similarly shining four piers frame the two sets of double bi-fold doors either side of the main single front door. Above the front door inset to the green tiles is a large, rectangular, ceramic name plate in glossy greens and yellows indicating the name of the bar, and with a juicy looking lemon cast in each corner. In the warmer weather the bi-fold doors on both sides of the bar are unlatched and creased back, opening the bar up to both Rue Garibaldi, with a view down to the market and at the front onto the large tree-lined square. Tables, chairs and parasols are placed on both pavement areas virtually doubling the size of the bar.

Hugo is the keeper of this bastion that is Le Petit Lemon. He is a large, barrel-chested, true Gallic soul with a thick mop of black wavy hair and a roughly cropped beard. Sprouting from his invisible top lip is a fabulous moustache, the extended fringes of which appear to disappear into his wide mouth. The flowing ends of the moustache extend and curl under his chubby cheeks. Hugo will often be seen proudly preening it with his garlic-sausage-like fingers, when deep in thought, or just for the hell of it. His bar uniform has always been a collarless white shirt, which always has the brass collar studs still attached, indicating that he did actually have detachable collars for the shirts. The shirts, sleeves rolled up, feel comfortable on his large upper body and also have the advantage of tenting his formidable girth. Those who got to know Hugo knew he could be as charming as any Frenchman could be when he wanted to as a host. But he could turn from the, normally, most hospitable, to the most uncouth and inhospitable in a fraction of a second. The bar was all his and within that domain no-one who either knew him or were first meeting him and looked into his dark, dark eyes would even consider crossing or upsetting him.

On first impression one might be fooled into thinking that Hugo could barely work the monstrous, chrome coffee machine that domi-nated the back of the bar, or turn out a portion of Croque Monsieur.

What only a few close associates knew, was that Hugo had, prior to his ownership of the bar, in fact, been a classically trained chef and possessed a deft skill over a hot stove. Historically, the downfall on his upward route to Michelin stardom had been because of what most great chef's suffer from; a lightning quick and frightening temper, and the total inability to accept any form of orders or discipline. You may consider that this is, in fact, an attribute to many great chefs but this trait had ultimately manifested itself in the two-Michelin-starred kitchen he was working in, in Marseille, fifteen years ago. Hugo had been drawn and baited, by the devilish, weasel like, sous chef working there, on a number of occasions over a period of months. It was suspected that this was only because his tormentor, in truth, was jealous of Hugo's culinary abilities. On the fateful day in question he had snapped after a sly, whispered comment by his impish tormentor about Hugo's crystal clear consommé being a fraction cloudy. Hugo had launched a butcher's cleaver at the despicable man, which fortunately had been horizontal in its rotating trajectory when it flew across the sous chef's head giving him a new and unwanted hair parting. The sympathetic restaurant owner, not wanting a fuss, had agreed to let Hugo go and paid the sous chef to not press charges. Since that time Hugo had never worked for anyone else; now he would always be his own boss.

Le Petit Lemon, as any bar in France and, in fact, most pubs in Great Britain, has a stock number of regular 'punters', as they are called in England. Those characters, who for varying reasons navigated to their familiar place: a place that was not home but felt like home, a place where they could be sociable or not sociable, where the bartender was like a wife or a husband, a confidant, someone who didn't judge them but would give them an opinion led judgement if they asked for it, a place where the world could be set right, where family problems could be aired, where politicians could be castigated with impunity. They will enter with all the issues and stresses that vex most each day and after some warming food and a glass or two of their preferred tipple, they would leave feeling as if they were not alone.

Maurice Corbin is one of these patrons and is small, in stature, even for a Frenchman. He undeniably would appear to most, more southern Mediterranean than French but had, in fact, lived his whole life in the town. His face has seen 65 years of local sun and has the patina and wrinkled grain of old burnished furniture; his dark hair colour peeping out from below his hat belies his age. Every day he wears the same garb, a small black Homburg hat, a black shirt with the sleeves rolled up, taupe coloured trousers and a pair of tan leather, wooden soled clogs that are a throw-back from the 1970s. You would be forgiven for thinking that each day Maurice wore the same clothes that were never laundered. But had anyone, other than his dear departed Amelie, ever ventured into his bedroom and opened the large stand-alone rococo wardrobe, they would see two other like hats on the shelf, six like shirts, laundered and pressed, four pairs of like trousers and two other pairs of like clogs all neatly arranged. Often Maurice would open the wardrobe in the early morning light and contemplate for a full three minutes, whilst rubbing his forehead what to wear. When Maurice returned to his small house at the same time every evening, had anyone but his dear departed Amelie seen him remove the Homburg, when he entered the bedroom, they would have seen the exact dividing line between darkly tanned and ivory skin on his forehead, where his hat had been lodged all day and which was only ever, ever removed when he went to bed.

Every day, however inclement, Maurice would sit outside Le Petit Lemon on *his* seat facing the square; a simply painted blue, pine dining chair which rested beside a weathered cast iron sewing machine stand with a marble table top, which had been drilled and adapted for a parasol. This seat no-one else ever sat on. Once an ill-fated Belgian tourist had ignorantly perched there with an expresso he had purchased from the bar, warmly confident that he had secured the best seat in the house. Before one savouring sip could be broached, Hugo had exited the bar, turfed the unsuspecting individual off the revered seat, removed the still steaming expresso from their quivering hand, muttered a few close up, menacingly deep, expletives and left the bemused Belgian to wander off with a distraught 'how did I offend' look on his face and questioning his own heritage.

Every day Maurice would sit and rest his back against the thick tiled wall, surrounded in season by trailing flowers from the various pots above. Each tile in the wall, irregularly fired, divided by thick layers of limed cement, were as individual as the characters of the small town. There Maurice would watch local and alien life go by, waiting to join his dearly departed Amelie but in no absolute hurry to do so. For Maurice there was still much traffic to watch passing, still much pastis and coffee to drink before noon, still much of the local wine, lapin and fromage to savour in the après-midi and evenings. None but a few had ever heard Maurice speak a conversational word apart from "Qui" and "Non" interposed with a grunt, the only other form of communication being a facial expression or a shrug.

A visiting elderly Parisian woman had once pulled a chair close to Maurice with her early morning degustation and tried to extract a conversation. This had been witnessed in amusement by Hugo. She spoke for forty five minutes solidly, often laughing at her own anecdotes, during which Maurice said nothing and continued to watch the street passages. When she eventually paused for breath and sighed, Maurice grunted and said "Non!" The woman got up, leaving her unfinished croissant, she walked off and was never seen again.

So Maurice would sit at his chair, table beside him, watching the three streets converge in the square. Strangely, he had never been seen to make any form of payment and yet in the morning Hugo would bring his first coffee and later his chilled pastis and small jug of water. It was cheese or cured meats with bread for luncheon and the vin du region throughout the afternoon and eventually, in the evening, Maurice would partake of a hot meal before leaving for home. It led the local conspiracy theorists in the town to believe that Maurice had some deep, dark hold over Hugo. Most didn't care for these theories.

Another of these permanent *residential* seats as you entered the bar is just inside the right far corner, against the wall. Any persons entering the bar with a security background would immediately have noticed that the position held a strategically strong position, with a view of the whole bar, the square and the Rue Garibaldi junction. Here sits Jacques Giroud; he is a short, dark skinned, gaunt man aged in his late forties. He has a permanently cropped head of dark, greying hair with numerous scars visible within the hairline and one on his left cheek. There's not an ounce of fat on his taut, sinewy body. His verdigris eyes appear to be fixed in a constantly manic stare even on the rare occasions when he smiles, though he has never been heard to laugh. The hushed rumour among the other regular patrons, that had long circulated the bar, was that Jacques had been a member of the revered French Foreign Legion in his younger days. As if to enhance this whisper, he has sometimes been heard to mutter

Arabic expletives when sitting at his table, drunk. In the evenings Jacques drinks only the magical green absinthe; many thought that this was what fuelled his vivid eyes. Certainly after the half bottle mark it had been noted, in the flickering candle light of his table that his eyes took on the same eerie glow as the liquid. For a man of such small stature he exuded an unsettling persona and even Hugo knew to be wary about discussing politics or any disastrous, historical French military endeavours with him. Everyone in the bar thought he was as crazy as a Parisian scooter commuter.

In total contrast to this image that Jacques inadvertently emitted, he was the proud owner of a dog; a white, miniature poodle called De Gaulle, after the country's great leader. The only distinguishing feature about De Gaulle that indicated he was a dog rather than a bitch was the large spiked collar he wore. This collar should have served as a warning to any who thought De Gaulle was an effeminate pooch. He had a fiery, snappy temper, that you could imagine mirrored his master's, and many uninitiated dog lovers had lost the skin and flesh off their hands to a whiplash rip of needle sharp teeth, when they inadvertently believed he required petting for some reason. De Gaulle would sit on a chair next to his owner at the small table. He did not need a lead as he was as obedient and disciplined as any military man. It was known that the only time he would leave his master's side was if an unwary customer in the bar left their glass of beer on a table while they visited the toilets. On these occasions the eagle-eyed De Gaulle would slink like a commando from his perch and weave between the tables to where the beer had been left, jump up on the chair with his front paws on the table and lap as much of the beer as he could before the customer returned. He would leave before being spotted and resume his seat beside his, now smiling, master, leaving the hapless beer owner to return and wonder whether they had in fact drunk that half a glass of chilled beer. For this reason De Gaulle was known, quite irreverently, as De Gaulle 'the Bastard'.

Since walking into Le Petit Lemon that numbing day Annabelle had left, Gerald had slowly become a familiar fixture with Hugo and the other regulars and, further, become part of the bar's familial congregation over the next two years. Of course in any small town community it is not just the regulars at a local bar or pub that a resident gets to know. A small town is similar in many ways to a bar. Some town residents have no character; visually they may be recognisable to other townsfolk and one may pass pleasantries with them in passing, but they are not memorable. There are, however, certain of the town's residents who remain etched in people's memories, dreams and even nightmares. Madame Chatnoir could be said to fit squarely in that more memorable category and not only with the town's human residents, but also with their pets and the feral animal's minds. Her name, to those who are mildly aware of the French language could well, either be related to good luck, or possibly some satanic following; in this case most believed the latter. Had Mme Chatnoir been alive in the 17th Century she would undoubtedly have been burnt at the stake in the market place, or 'ducked' in the nearby river until drowned and proven innocent, or floated and then burnt anyway. If anything dispelled doubts about her links to the dark arts it was the fact that, even though she was in her late 70s, she had the spectral ability to move about the town as if by some ancient enchantment. Permanent residents were only too aware of her abilities and some had inherited a sixth sense when it came to moving about the town at night. Those who were not born there, however, often had to gain that extra sense from experience.

As stated, the residents of the town weren't the only ones to suffer from Mme Chatnoir's phantom-like status. For, unlike her surname suggested, if there was one thing she hated more than foreigners and processed cheese, it was cats. Many of the multitude of feline residents that padded around the town's darkened streets at night had been caught out by Madame's un-paralleled furtive stealth. Her ability to be able to lodge most of her big toe out of the front of her nun-like sandals, up the poor, unenlightened animal's rectum and hoof it to wheelie bin height with a speed, which again, belied her age, was renowned among the tight-knit cat community. On the odd occasion when Mme Chatnoir had not seen a cat on her nocturnal wanderings she had often surprised the local urban fox. On one occasion a very short gentleman from the north of the town, who it has to be stated, did have fox-like features, stooped to tie his shoe lace and had suffered the same uncomfortable and surprising sensation that many a cat had before him.

Gerald had, on a number of occasions in his early residency, walked home from the square down a visibly well-lit thoroughfare, turned his head for a split second, then resumed his gaze to be caught out by Mme Chatnoir standing right next to him. She had just appeared, standing, arms folded, with a half-smile on her wrinkled face. Peering out from the black scarf that shrouded the rest of her head, she was standing right beside a solid, impenetrable wall, with no visible means of having got there and all in that minuscule instant that Gerald had averted his previously calm gaze. The ensuing adrenalin rush and accompanying *girly* cry from Gerald had unfortunately meant he had had to return at speed to Le Petit Lemon for another drink until his heart had reduced its beating to a sufficiently safe rate. Hugo, on seeing him the first few times returning to the bar, knew exactly what had befallen Gerald. He had tried to describe who this local apparition was but Gerald's ashen stare indicated he was not comprehending so Hugo had steeled him with a small brandy and eventually allowed him to re-make his wary way home to try and find peaceful slumber.

Chapter Three

The Monk's Chambers

Most of the streets in the older part of the town where Gerald lived were very similar: each house was in a different state of repair: individual wrought iron grilles on the windows and some doors, each house a slightly different shade of washed colour, weathered render going through various states of the peeling process, different sized windows, some with battered storm shutters, some without, but still showing the remnants of cast hinges where they had previously been. Some houses had been modernised, but their core frame, as with Mme Joella's, having been in situ from the beginnings of the castled town and dating back to the beginning of the seventeenth century. Every front door was as diverse as the interior dwelling it guarded. So it was when Mme Joella's street doors were opened. Her street doors were the original gnarled and cracked double doored, portico type, with a large rusty black iron knob and huge escutcheon covering the keyhole for the four-inch iron key on the opening side. The other closed door had not been opened since Mme Joella could recall and the hinges and iron bolts and nails wept red streams down the thick, patinated timbers. Entering past these doors one would step through a deep archway, bordered by ornate, dilapidated stonework that modern masons would struggle to create. This led into a small twenty pace, square courtyard, open to the sky above and bordered by the next door property to the right-hand aspect and Mme Joella's vast house to the three other sides. The courtyard walls had been painted by Mme Joella in a pale blue to about twelve feet, the height she could reach and roughly squared off with an extendable brush, above this gave way to the original dull render. On the floor was an uneven pattern of the original huge flagstones, which appeared to have been polished but were only so through the constant use of human traffic. On these sat small wheelie bins mingled with the various sized potted plants Mme had dotted about and then left to their own devices. Various sized windows were obscurely placed in random parts of the inner walls facing out from Mme Joella's numerous apartments in the substantial residence. On the far left of the courtyard were two stone steps leading to a further large, but less weathered set of thick wooden doors with six ornate panels each inset with fine black scrolled ironwork. These doors were always open and led into a small ante entrance made up of a white wooden glazed framework; each of the glazed panels were of beautiful antique etched and coloured water glass. Beyond this a small door in the inner porch led into the dark, inner hall and the monumental stone stairwell. Notably, the handle on this door, that Gerald had to use each day, was antique and depicted the form of a hand clutching a large truncheon. Gerald disliked this handle as it reminded him how often he had been *under the cosh* with Annabelle. The staircase was formed from bespoke slabs of granite that were supported by the classic arched forms that would have graced any castle. It rose four floors, interspersed with large landings, culminating at the intricate plaster cornice and centre rose that adorned the ceiling in the foyer to Gerald's apartment's front door on the top floor.

Gerald's apartment was one of two loft conversions in the top of the ancient house. A large structural timber beam ran across it that, although painted primrose yellow, was at such a height that Gerald was forever hitting his head on it. The main living area spanned either side of this antagonistic lintel. At the far end, the door on the left led to a compact but bright kitchenette decorated in red and white with matching utensils and tea towels; beyond that was a shower and laundry room with the huge hot water cylinder standing in the corner. On the opposite side of the lounge to this was the doorway to Gerald's *Monk's Chamber*, as he had so named it; he thought it fitting as both he and his brethren monks were vowed to celibacy. It was graced with a large double bed and a table and chair beside the door to the bijou balcony. To get into bed Gerald would have to slide from the bottom to the top of the bed to out-fox the sloping ceiling that followed the roof rafters and ran down to the head of the bed. Gerald had often, annoyingly, sat up in the morning and wedged his head, requiring a contortionist move to extricate his wiry body from between the ceiling and the soft mattress.

Most of the apartment was daubed with the same warm yellow emulsion which reflected the almost daily warm sunshine that flowed in from the windows which all looked out of the same far roof top aspect. The windows in the apartment were lower than you could see out of so, in effect, Gerald had to sit on a chair or the bed to get a view. One of the benefits of the loft apartment for Gerald was that once he was ensconced in his home he could wander around naked with no chance of offending any of his neighbours 15 feet across the street.

The exception to the limited view was the balcony, which sat in a dormer of the Mansard style roof and allowed Gerald to drag one chair and a small table out from the lounge to get his view across the neighbouring street's roofs. Gerald had always been intrigued by this view; although each property ascended from the street squarely for four or five levels, the roof-tops were as random as the number of degrees on a protractor. All were layered with the beautiful pale pink and peach arched tiles reminiscent of the colour of Cotes de Provence wine. The gradients of each tiled slope to their apexes, pitched and rolled like a rippling rosé sea in a light breeze. Little used and crumbling chimney stacks protruded to varying heights above these waves, and barely held the rusty poles with wire braces which were supporting numerous television aerials. Some of the chimneys shone like old aluminium funnels being purely maintained by the aid of copious amounts of silver flashing tape wrapped around the whole structure. Gerald always thought the whole scene gave the impression of a vast fleet of ships that had long been scuttled in a blush lagoon. Below the roofline under the little worked, broken, cast iron and ceramic gutters were draped a myriad of cables, supplying the mains electricity, telephones and sometimes nothing at all, twisted loosely across the streets below.

The narrow streets of the small town, to some, could seem almost claustrophobic. If it wasn't for the architectural strength of the continuous, individual five storey buildings, it might seem as if they were falling in on the small thoroughfares. The consequence of this topography was that when the blistered shutters were pinned back from the open windows in the long, hot seasons, every word spoken, every chair drawn back, every footstep on polished Pamment tile, every creaking bone and other such human noises could be heard by the whole street. Lifelong residents even knew where each sound emanated from. Conversations could be held all evening with other residents without leaving home or even seeing the other party.

At 7am every morning the small church clock in the main street would chime its seven tolls. For some reason unknown to all the residents, five minutes later it would re-chime all seven again, often leaving the uninitiated with a horrible feeling of *deja vu*. Each morning, Gerald would lay prostate on his extra-large bed, alone as usual. He has lived in this small apartment built into the eves of the beautiful old 17th Century townhouse, which he had rented from Mme Joella, and originally with Annabelle, for the past three and a half years. He was usually still in that state of half sleep, that disposition that everybody desires, until wakefulness takes hold. His skinny body would still be attempting to dissipate the past evening's reasonably priced, but excellent, glasses of plummy Bordeaux. In his semi-conscious state he would be aware of the shuffling footsteps of Maurice making his way to the town square, up the Rue Palais below Gerald's room. As the last chime of the second set rang out, Maurice would pause in his step, pass wind loudly and then continue in his passage as if nothing had happened. Gerald still in slumber would retort, "Bonjour Maurice!", which was heard by Maurice and the rest of the residents of the street who were awake. Maurice would normally just grunt but not break his step towards his destination outside Le Petit Lemon. And so this scenario played out nearly every morning at exactly that same time. To Gerald it was as an alarm call; his time to greet a new day.

Gerald would sit on his balcony, normally naked, in the early mornings and muse about the scene and other things with his first mug of tea—tea that had never been the same since he had left England, no matter what brand he bought. This is how he would start his days, staring across at the canted landscape and below, to his slim view of the narrow junction at Rue de la Republique and Rue Palais. In the evenings he would sit and warm his naked body on the balcony from the residual heat that had been soaked up by the roof tiles opposite. Gerald would often pour a cold glass of wine and listen to one of the three vinyl albums he owned: Brook Benton, Lou Rawls or Etta James played on the large, wooden Garrard music centre which took up one wall in the lounge and acted as a side table and 1960s entertainment centre.

Gerald had become somewhat of a reasonable cook since living in the apartment without Annabelle, having found an old basic cookery book on the shelves of the rented apartment. The lack of fast food and take-away restaurants in the town had really quite forced his hand, however. His evening routine would see him pour a glass of wine, slip a record onto the gramophone, tie on his grey and white striped butcher's apron over his naked self and prepare the fresh ingredients bought from the supermarche, then cook his meal. The apron was, in effect, just there to stop any important parts of his physique getting burnt or splashed with hot fat; to the rear of the apron his pale buttocks were fully exposed. He would then shower, dress and go to Le Petit Lemon to see his few friends for another drink and social discourse and to set the world, according to Clairville, right.

Chapter Four

Domaine Saint Patrice

The Domaine Saint Patrice, where Gerald had gained employment, is a very well respected vineyard, which sits four miles from Clairville. It nestles in the undulating hills with far reaching views of the rock escarpment and Clairville. It is a historic vineyard which passed into the hands of the De Beauvoir family in the late 1800s. It is still a principle employer in the area and many of the local residents have worked there all their lives. Although they produce their own wines, principally the dry, glowing, pale amber rosé, they send the majority of their produce to the local cooperative vintner for mass production of the Languedoc region wines.

Gerald had worked there for five months prior to Annabelle's surprise departure. In conjunction with the support from Hugo and the regulars at Le Petit Lemon, the vineyard work had assisted Gerald in dealing with his heartache, his grief. Gerald needed routine; like so many other human beings, he found solace in being tasked. It gave him a reason to get up every day and breathe. He would arrive promptly at the vineyard every morning in Bella and get lost, during the winter months in pruning, and collecting the cuttings for composting, tilling the rough soil around the vine stems that were older than he, and then in the early spring he would join the throng in gently nurturing the fruits, ready for harvesting and sorting them for the different wines, the best for the house wines and the rest for the co-operative blends.

As time went on Gerald became friendly with the head vintner, Jules, who, in Gerald's down time would explain in his best English how the grapes were to be handled and pulped, slowly introducing him to the filtration and ageing processes in the vats and then the transfer to the ageing barrels. Gerald found the processes enthralling. He visited the main library at Beziers and began to read about the various processes in the many regions of the country. In time he became familiar with the basic vintner's craft and Jules would allow him to assist with some of the more menial vintner's roles around the vineyard. Gerald thrived on the responsibility and found himself immersed within the winemaker's craft.

Now, it has to be said, the majority of the employees at Domaine Saint Patrice are not young. Principally they are men—old men; in this particularly traditional area of France, the men worked the vines. In contrast, in the picking season, many young students would arrive and stay in the meagre accommodation lodges, to work, picking a few bunches of grapes in order to briefly tick a box on their curriculum vitae before setting off to 'maid' in the European ski chalets for the following season. But in the main, the older men of the region worked the vines. Gerald was, in fact, a young man compared to a lot of the other male employees.

The owner of the Domaine Saint Patrice is Madame Cecilly De Beauvoir. Her great grandfather, Phillipe De Beauvoir, had, allegedly, won the vineyards from a wealthy nobleman in a game of chance at the casino in Marseille. Mme Cecilly, as she had always wanted to be known, had taken the reins in running the vineyards just after the second world war. Her devotion to the St Patrice name was matched only by her love of horses, fashion and men. Taking the reins was more than just a metaphor; she ran the vineyards with a rod of iron, but in Mme Cecilly's case it was a vintage riding crop. Many employees in her fifty year reign had felt the crack of her crop on their bodies, whether in anger or, more often than not, passion. No-one knew how old she was, but it could be surmised that she was in her early eighties. She had been a good friend of Coco Chanel and so had an enormous wardrobe of friend Coco's clothing that she wore most days as her everyday garb.

Mme Cecilly had been a beauty in her day. Her small athletic frame, high pronounced cheekbones, soft face, mass of auburn hair and of course, the fact that she was heir to a large, financially secure vineyard had made her the target of very many amorous advances from wealthy men, actors, racing drivers and politicians. Although there had been some long term affairs she had never married. The truth was that throughout all of these liaisons her huge sexual appetite had worn most of her suitors out. This appetite had never waned and as she aged her suitors had also diminished and therefore Mme Cecilly had turned her attentions to the many men who worked for her at the vineyards and in the stables where her string of thoroughbred horses were retained. The majority of the men in her employ were in their late fifties and sixties and all had been 'ridden' by Mme Cecilly at some stage in their employment. Most believed, or saw it as part of their contract of employment.

In her younger years Mme Cecilly would trot around the estate on one of her prized horses, crop in hand, but over time and now, much to her annoyance, her more frail ageing body did not have the endurance to get in or out of the saddle, or to stay on. Consequently she had purchased a brand new two-seat golf buggy some years ago. This had been vinyl wrapped in the familiar gold and bronze Louis Vuitton colours and the fabric roof and seats trimmed in the same luscious material at her behest. This ancillary work had cost as much as the primary cost of the buggy and it was now her main transport around the estate. Mme Cecilly would tour the vineyard daily, the gentle whine of the buggy motor sending the old men hobbling for cover in the neat rows of vines. Madame's make-up was applied more heavily now; she would inevitably be dressed in one of her Chanel ensembles, her slight frame causing the tailored clothing to drape now, rather than fit perfectly. Her silk stockings were slightly wrinkled on her spindly, skinny legs, the infamous horse crop sitting in its bespoke holder on the side of the windscreen frame, ready to be drawn at a moment's notice.

Gerald had met Mme Cecilly when he was originally employed by Jules. Gerald couldn't help but notice the way Mme Cecilly had looked him up and down with her, still bright blue eyes. He was one of the younger employees and he assumed the vineyard owner was checking his wiry physique to satisfy herself that he could carry out the hard vineyard work. The vineyard manager Jules, knew exactly what was happening and always felt a pang of conscience at not pre-warning any new employ-ees about their potential extraneous duties that lay ahead.

The employees at the vineyard were expected to work on the vines and grounds, assist with the wine making processes under the steer of Jules, and assist with looking after the horses in the large stable block. The stable block is a large historic building set in a 'T' shape; it is a two storey building with the same facade as the main Chateau Saint Patrice. The ground floor is set aside for the 30 stalls and large central tack rooms and store. Above are the accommodation areas, that in the past, had been for the chateau's numerous staff. These rooms mainly lay dormant now, occasionally used by visiting casual labourers during the picking season.

On a particularly warm and sunny spring day Gerald was sent to the stable house to assist with cleaning the tack room and stables. Part way through his morning he had stripped to his vest as he was hot mucking out the five stalls that had been in use. Gerald had been surprised to find he was the only person Jules had sent to the stables that day but got on with the job in hand anyway. He didn't hear the gentle hum of the designer buggy as it approached up the central aisle of the stable block. He also didn't hear Mme Cecilly approach and stand for a full four minutes watching his labour from behind her large black Chanel sunglasses. Gerald's peripheral vision noticed the light pink check of Mme Cecilly's tweed suit and he span around in surprise.

"Madame," he said, clearly shocked, as he stood up straight with his hay fork as if to attention.

"Monsieur Gerald, I was hoping to catch you here, to welcome you properly to Chateau Saint Patrice." Her English pronunciation was perfect, but with her slight French accent. "Walk with me for a moment please Gerald; you don't mind if I call you Gerald, do you?"

"No, no, of course Madame," Gerald replied.

He went to grab his shirt from the stall wall but Mme Cecilly said,

"That's fine, Gerald; you're fine as you are." Gerald complied and left his shirt and the fork in the stable. "Let me give you a tour of the stable block, it has much history. I love the smells here, the fresh hay, my fillies and stallions and the sweat of the men working hard," she continued. Gerald thought his employer's last comment was strange but quickly attributed it to her being French.

The first floor was reached via a beautiful galleried staircase, befitting of the monumental stable block. Mme Cecilly expounded on how many famous faces had toured the stables back in the day as she clearly drifted off reminiscing about her halcyon days, pointing out photographs of some of the people she mentioned that were adorning the hallways. They came to a large set of mahogany double doors. Mme Cecilly retrieved a large-cast key from her jacket pocket, and unlocked and opened the left hand door. She stepped inside the salon and beckoned Gerald in.

"Please take a seat, Gerald," she said quietly turning the latch on the key to lock the door without Gerald noticing. "I like to get to know all my employees, Gerald. Please take a seat," she purred as she wafted across the room to the drinks trolley beside the fireplace.

Gerald took a seat on one of the two large settees facing each other laterally to the fireplace. Gerald sat on the edge of the seat, clearly uncomfortable and not wanting to look too relaxed in the company of his employer. Mme Cecilly poured two large glasses of the pinot noir in the decanter on the trolley. She walked over and handed Gerald the glass and then sat on the settee opposite him in a far more relaxed posture.

"Please, relax; drink, Gerald. This is us informally getting to know each other." She smiled and touched her glass to her mouth, just letting the light wine wet her glossy red lips. Similar to a yawn, Gerald unconsciously copied and raised his glass to his mouth and quaffed two large mouthfuls. Within minutes he felt more relaxed and eased back in to the large cushions which enveloped him, smiling at Mme Cecilly. Later, Gerald remembered her harking back to her past more and he recalled she had commented on how toned his muscles appeared to be for his age.

Sometime later Gerald awoke with a start in the stable he had been cleaning. He jumped to his feet knocking the hay fork to the ground with a clatter, pulling his shirt off the wall. His immediate thought was concern that he may have been caught sleeping on the job by his employers. He looked at the large clock above the distant tack room—a quarter to five in the afternoon. He recalled Mme Cecilly coming to see him and the tour of the first floor but after that he could remember nothing. Another thought then flooded into his head—he was bursting to go for a pee. He rushed to the stable toilet block but as he got to face the toilet and undid his zipper he couldn't find the button flies on his boxer shorts. He span around and tore his trousers and boxers down, sitting heavily on the toilet seat he peed just in time like a proverbial dray horse. Sighing loudly he noticed two things next. Firstly his boxer shorts were on back to front. Well no wonder you couldn't find the buttons you idiot, he thought. Then, secondly, the waxy red substance that appeared to be coming off his penis as he dabbed it dry with toilet paper. Gerald checked the roll of toilet paper. Nothing on the paper. Did he rinse properly in the shower that morning? What the hell was it? As he mused this development he stood up to pull his now correctly positioned boxers up. As he did so he flinched with pain as his fingers crossed a sore area on his buttocks. Gerald shuffled out to the handbasin area with his trousers around his ankles and turned to point his back to the large mirrored area above the sinks. He focussed and looked quizzically at the two perfect red wheals in the shape of an 'X' across his bum. He touched the raised area and flinched again at the tenderness of the area. "What the hell!" he said to himself.

An hour and thirty minutes later Gerald sat at the bar in Le Petit Lemon and poured Hugo a glass of wine from his plastic milk container. He explained to his confidant his strange afternoon's events. Hugo smiled and chuckled to himself. Gerald looked at him quizzically.

"I believe you have been branded my friend; you are now a member of Mme Cecilly's personal stud." Hugo explained in more detail how many of the male employees at Domaine Saint Patrice had also experienced a loss of all time. He explained further about Mme Cecilly's expert use of Keratin, learnt from the stable's veterinarian—one of her earlier conquests. Gerald listened aghast as Hugo explained that this was all normal at Domaine Saint Patrice.

Four miles away in the salon of the stable block, a fire now roared in the hearth and Mme Cecilly crossed to a panel on the wood clad walls, pressing and sliding the hidden door to one side she placed the VHS tape in her hand, simply labelled 'Gerald', on the shelf next to the numerous other tapes. A small brass plaque pinned to the leading edge of the shelf was simply engraved 'Mes etalons'. She walked towards the fire and took her glass from the mantle, sipping the warm red wine with a smile of satisfaction.

Chapter Five

The 5k Run

It was a sunny, Sunday morning and just after Maurice's alarm call, Gerald was sitting at his balcony table with his pot of tea, contemplating the day ahead. Mme Joella had requested help with a few simple DIY jobs, but otherwise the day was his. In amongst the background music Gerald was listening to on his ageing radio, he suddenly became aware of the sound of running footsteps; someone late for the boulangerie, possibly? Gerald adjusted his gaze to the small junction below his balcony and the sound of many footsteps which were growing in volume, voices talking and echoing in amongst purposeful breathing. Then the first of the fluorescent, lycra clad runners breezed through, heading towards the main square. The obviously regular runners in their expensive designer running apparel, made to keep their lithe, shiny bodies cool when hot and breaking a sweat; €200 running shoes supporting arches on a bed of air-filled rubber as they pounded the cobbled streets. As the athletes passed, so the more amateur runners jogged through, past Gerald's interested gaze. All shapes and sizes in varying degrees of fitness and dress, until bringing up the rear of the caravan were the families, mothers jogging with sporty push-chairs and the downright unfit who were now walking at a quickened pace. Long since having given up jogging after only 150 metres from the start of the 5k run, which had begun in the square earlier that morning. some, inevitably, wouldn't make it at all,

Gerald, his interest sparked, had thrown on some shorts and a tee shirt and forgetting to brush his teeth, dashed down the four flights of stone stairs to investigate what was happening in the square. Getting into the swing of things Gerald jogged in his flip flops to the square to find a small crowd gathered around Monsieur Dumas, the owner of the local cycling shop. Gerald greeted all he knew cordially and picked up one of the leaflets from the makeshift decorating table that Monsieur Dumas sat behind. He read; it was a 5k *fun* run in aid of the local community charities. Simply gather some sponsorship, complete the run, have a good time and the local good causes benefited. What could be better! Gerald recalled he had cut quite a dashing figure in his youth, during school sports day. He had finished fourth in his end of year mile dash at the school. He hadn't put on much weight since then and he'd kept reasonably active and, after all, it was only 5k. If mothers with push-chairs could do it he thought, then why not me? The next race was planned for Sunday, two weeks hence. He would enter. Monsieur Dumas saw the glint in Gerald's eye and questioned,

"Et tous, Gerald?"

Gerald stared back at him sternly and said

"Qui!"

Gerald made for home after completing the simple signing on form. In his thoughts he mused what better way to impress his admiring but sometimes mocking comrades at Le Petit Lemon. He would have to practice, he thought, as he entered the street door to home. In his apartment he rummaged through his wardrobe and some boxes of, as yet, unpacked clothes. He had nothing to wear! As he showered he recalled the nearby decathlon sporting superstore had been advertising a sale in the local paper and, better still, it was open on Sundays.

A short bus ride later that morning, and he was in the huge sporting warehouse where you could buy anything from saddle sore cream to a canoe to a pair of socks. Gerald headed straight to the reduced sale department. He stared up at the expansive posters of rippling, bronzed young people running up an endless road in the very newest apparel—breathable lycra. Gerald became intoxicated, for a change by something else—by the whole fitness *thing*. He rifled through the racks of and leggings and tops until he found just the thing, a fluorescent fitted yellow vest; after all he'd want to be seen. Rummaging further he found a very sporty, tight, pair of three quarter length shorts. After a short session in the changing facility, Gerald looked in the mirror and he was impressed with how the lycra actually made him look younger, almost like the men in the posters—yes he could carry this look off. He headed towards the check-out pausing only to pick up a cheap pair of running shoes that did match his vest but would probably do little to enhance his running prowess. He paid and caught the bus back home.

Over the next two weeks, on a nightly basis, Gerald went out jogging a route around the streets, slowly increasing his distances. After all he wanted his friends to think he was already fit and had just competed in the race *ad hoc*. On his nightly sojourn he only came across a couple of surprised local residents and on turning into one rue had been nearly caught by Madame Chatnoir where Gerald swore he felt the draft as her left foot passed by his buttocks. Gerald actually took a positive slant from this, that his speed must have increased recently in order for Madame Chatnoir to, uncharacteristically, miss the target. He sprinted the rest of the way home.

On the morning of the run the azure skies were clear and a light breeze filtered through the curtains of Gerald's apartment. Perfect running weather! Unfortunately, on this Sunday, Gerald had slept in. As he suddenly became conscious of the time he flew as quickly as his ageing bones would allow to the lounge where he had his running kit laid out ready. He slipped into his shorts and did his shoes up slipping his vest over his head. He neglected to brush his hair and unaccustomedly, didn't check his look in the mirror. He walked quickly from the apartment and jogged down the stairs, two at a time.

Unfortunately for Gerald, what he had assumed were hi-tech running shorts were in fact knee length cycling shorts. Had he actually been seen by any of his friends in the weeks prior he would have probably been educated to this fact as road cycling is France's sport second only to football. As a consequence, sewn into the rear gusset of these particular shorts were two *squidgy* gel ridges that ran parallel to the centre seam of the crutch for about three inches. Any cyclist would know that these pudgy crests were to be worn to the back to protect one's bony posterior from the ravages of a hard, narrow racing bike seat and rough roads. Gerald had, rightly, assumed these pads were to aid comfort, possibly to reduce chaffing whilst running, but not which way round they should be worn. This morning Gerald had pulled them on in his haste and hadn't noticed that they were prominently at the front.

Gerald entered the already bustling square at a jog and ran on the spot in front of Monsieur Dumas at the signing on table. Monsieur Dumas ticked Gerald off on his list and looking him up and down, particularly knowingly at his shorts, smiled and said, "Tres bon Gerald, tres bon!".

Gerald took this as a compliment and slowly but still jogging on the spot, moved over to where some of the more professional looking runners were gathering. A small crowd was congregating outside Le Petit Lemon for an early refreshment, all of whom knew Gerald. There was certainly a buzz of conversation amongst them as they watched Gerald warming up. He looked from the corner of his eye and he was pleased with the obvious enamoured gazes and finger pointing of his friends. Hugo exited the bar on hearing the sound of excited conversation, and immediately had his gaze directed to the very bright, tight, figure of Gerald stretching, bending and hip swivelling. Wanting only to get a better look, Hugo dashed back into the bar and very quickly returned carrying a tray with a large measure of pastis, a glass and a very small jug of water. He walked in amongst the throng of runners and over to Gerald.

"Zheral, pour le vigour, eh!" Hugo boomed.

"Oh! Merci, Hugo", Gerald retorted.

He took the large pastis and poured what little water he could into it and began to down it. Gerald noticed, and was a little disconcerted by his friend's smiling gaze at his legs in lycra but particularly at the crotch area. Gerald was pleased that he had taken the time, as ever the modest gentleman, to tuck his penis and associated tackle down under and in between his legs, in the tight material.

The early morning aniseed infusion certainly seemed to work; Gerald felt invigorated. Hugo returned to the bar with the empty glass held high to applause from the small crowd of patrons. He immediately went to his telephone.

The race began to an unexpected cheer from the growing crowd outside Le Petit Lemon, which made all the competitors, and especially Gerald, think that this was something special. They twisted and turned down the narrow streets. Gerald, full of confidence, attempted to maintain pace with the lead pack. After about 500 metres Gerald felt that the pastis was now having an altered and derogatory effect on his performance. Half way down Rue Montmarche another small crowd had gathered outside Le Bleu Bistro. Pre-warned by Hugo they had a small chilled carafe of red wine and a large glass waiting. The small host cheered and beckoned to Gerald, who by this point believed a short *breather* might be advantageous. He ran over in a sprightly manner. The large glass of cold Bergerac was thrust into his athletic hand and his friends gestured for him to quaff, rather than sip his refreshment. Gerald, always a believer in the 'hair of the dog' principle obliged and soaked up the admiring stares at his attire by the gathered throng. And so it was for the next three and a half kilometres. Not a street went by without Gerald being accosted or called to either a makeshift bar outside a house or one of the other numerous licensed premises along the route. After about four hours, Gerald jogged unsteadily back towards the town square, followed by a gaggle of cheering and encouraging children. If this sort of fan base and following could be gleaned in this amateur event, perhaps he should consider joining a veteran athletics team, he thought, rather blearily.

As he reached the square he saw that the race had long since finished but he was greeted by what seemed like the whole town cheering for him; he felt like an Olympian, a hero. Some well-wishers had hastily ripped down a string of bunting stretched across the road to make an impromptu finishing line. Gerald, feeling the airs of a champion, put on a final gangly sprint and ran through the finish line raising his arms and spinning around in mock triumph. This afforded all those gathered a superb view of the now infamous lycra shorts. It seemed as if the whole town was in the square and, if it was at all possible, a greater cheer rang out. Gerald's efforts and his shorts gave rise to a day-long celebration outside Le Petit Lemon which ran long into the sunny afternoon and dusky evening. The crowds eventually dwindled away and after much back-slapping, selfie photographs with Gerald, incomprehensible compliments in the bar, and another uncomfortable moment when he was hugged by Hugo, Gerald eventually trudged his weary, drunk, aerobicist body home. Having negotiated the staircase, which really did appear and feel like it was in fact ten storeys, he went straight to his bedroom, surprisingly managing to duck the beam on the way. In the half light of his bed side lamp Gerald pulled off his top to admire his new runner's physique in front of his dressing mirror. With a glazed view he looked down proudly at his new shorts; he saw, and as he saw he realised, and as he realised, he uttered loudly

"Oh! Mon dieu, I have a vagina!"

Gerald collapsed backwards, fast asleep before he even hit the bed. Through the open windows and down the narrow street those who were aware sniggered in their slumber. Those who were not, lay aghast and wide eyed. The following morning there was a small parcel of lycra in Mme Joella's plastic recycling bin.

Chapter Six

Bella's Veneration

In the summer season the three sister towns on the raised topography above the Mediterranean plain, held their night markets. This was a relatively recent fashion which undoubtedly developed due to the influx of cash rich tourists who enjoyed nothing better than mixing with the locals over a glass or two of wine and the opportunity to peruse the local wares, foods and crafts in the comfort of a warm town square. In order not to encroach on each other's profits and to maximise the nightly visitors the towns held their markets on consecutive mid-week Tuesday, Wednesday and Thursday nights. It gave the various micro trades the ability to sell their products in amongst the various wine producers and food providers. So, in effect, one could enter the square at 6pm, view all the local crafts for sale at various stalls, whilst sipping a chilled rosé in a plastic cup. Later, one could purchase some hot meat off the boucherie's stainless steel roasting pit, get a side of plantain or paella, and wash it down with more wine. This could be followed by sampling a dessert; maybe the locally grown raspberries carefully moulded into a crunchy, chewy, creamy roulade, with yet more wine. Then settle back with the convivial crowd to listen and dance to an aspiring local band on the square's stage; and yes—more wine!

Far from being the domain of the yearly influx of tourists, the locals also enjoyed the three nightly festivities in the warmer months, often travelling between the three towns to socialise, chat with old friends and make new ones. Gerald was one of the loyal patrons; early in his lonely days after Annabelle had taken her leave he would drive the 5 to 10 kilometres between his home to the other two towns to enjoy the company of other resident *ex pats* and British tourists who made the vigil to the market squares. Unfortunately one of these such trips, in the last year, was where Gerald, had, as usual, driven his ageing, grey Renault 4, Bella, to Bezille the nearest market to his own town. He had sat for the evening at a trestle table and been swept up in a red wine frenzy with a particularly funny Yorkshireman called Keith, and his buxom wife. On conversing, the couple stated that they were in the area looking to buy a property. Gerald had said he would be happy to help them with the area which he knew well. The end of the night came all too soon after a few too many dances with Keith's wife, who appeared to enjoy dancing with her hands tightly gripping Gerald's buttocks; This only seemed to make Keith laugh even louder than he had all night.

Gerald had eventually swayed back to his beloved Bella after many handshakes and hugs from Keith and his wife. It was whilst sitting in Bella trying to get the key into the tricky ignition, which had been fitted under the steering column by some previous owner, that there had been a tap on the window. Gerald had looked up with a smile and a glazed stare into the face of a returning smile from Officer Laroux. Gerald had apologised to Officer Laroux and tried, in his best *Franglais,* to explain how difficult it was to get the ignition key into the inaccessible hole. Needless to say, after a short stint at the local police station, Gerald had been sent on his, still merry, pedestrian way by the officer and his sergeant. Two days later Gerald had eventually returned and got Bella back to the tree lined parking spot in the square near Le Petit Lemon. He had not driven her again, up to the time two weeks later when he lost his licence to drive and also gained a substantial fine in the nearby magistrate's court. Gerald was subsequently made aware by Hugo that had he been caught by the nearby State Police he would undoubtedly have ended up incarcerated for a good number of months as well as losing his licence and as a result he was ever grateful to Officer Laroux, who he, ironically, often shared a drink with in the bars of Bezille.

From that day Bella had sat in the same parking space in the square; everyone knew the story and she was left unmolested and in peace, by the local residents. This was, however, apart from the native, nightly roosting pigeons and starlings who had turned the poor little automobile into somewhat of a landmark. The grey and white droppings from above had slowly splattered, layered, formed and crusted over the whole car for the last year, giving the totally encased Bella the impression that she was in fact a perfect, one to one scale, clay model. Appreciation for the new town statue varied until it came to be an 'in or out' question. The regular users of the square, adored it's *Frenchness* and how it acted as a stark reminder of the follies of drinking and driving. Others, mostly of the few well to do in the town, cited her as a health risk. It was true that poor Bella could give off a smell not unlike a cave occupied by a million bats on some warm days and Hugo would have to approach with a towel around his face and spray her with copious amounts of his lavender floor spray.

The well to do contingent of the town had asked their local gendarme, Officer Martin, why it had not been subject to parking restrictions and the national *scrappage* scheme. He had shrugged and typically, left the matter in such a way that it left the question totally unresolved. They then wrote to their incumbent local councillor , Jean Pickles, who, in a sweat and influenced by the more affluent authors, had tried to get the vehicle removed. As a result there had been such an outcry from the majority of his electorate in this small catchment and, this being in his year for re-election, he had eventually rescinded any such order. In fact, after a meeting with his weaselly campaign secretary, Andre, he had decided to enhance his ballot box responses by calling a press conference in the town square in front of Bella.

Jean Pickles stood at the wooden lectern, set up in the square, draped in the red, white and blue tricolour rosettes, as the local press cameras whirred and flashed. Jean is not a small man and had taken to wearing light coloured linen suits which, unfortunately, accentuated all the areas that Mssr. Pickles sweats from. Standing right beside Bella, who had been deodorised in anticipation, he dramatically fanned himself with one of his own flyers and extolled the virtues of the innovation and creativity of the unknown artist who had placed this iconic image of French automobile history in just the right place to utilise the otherwise unwanted bird excrement so cleverly. This was much to the amusement of the patrons of Le Petit Lemon who gathered around and cheered at his discourse. Spurred on by this clamour he went further to proclaim that it would be a travesty, a crime against art, should anything happen to Bella. The gathered throng of townsfolk and journalists hurrahed at the wonderful yet preposterous scene and, as if to place a seal on the proclamation, a large pigeon who had been sitting in the tree above Pickles sent a large package of poop down to splatter on the left shoulder of his beige Hugo Boss suit. There was a brief gasp, then Pickles, who knew how to play a crowd, held his arms out smiled, uncomfortably, and shouted "Et Voila!". The crowd went crazy and Pickles winked to the nearby Andre. Such was the success of Pickles' efforts that he was invited by Hugo to carry on campaigning in Le Petit Lemon until the early hours of the following morning. Meanwhile, Bella's keys had been left hanging in Gerald's apartment ever since to remind him not to be so stupid in the future.

The incident had not excluded Gerald from the markets, however. He often hitched a lift from a friend, or caught a bus, when they ran, to enable him to get to the midweek socials. He had often been too late to get a lift home but had found to his surprise that the silent, starlit walk back to his home town had been a fitting cap to a lovely night. However it was to be another 12 months until Gerald was even able to try and get his licence back, and even then he would have to re-test. Gerald knew, at some time, something would have to be done about his transport arrangements. That time came one Monday morning when he was sitting on his balcony with his tea and a fresh croissant perusing La Cote Gazette, a free local paper that came most weekends with some district news but was predominantly advertisements. Gerald's eyes were captivated by one such particular advert. He took his spectacles off and cleaned them with the steam from his tea and napkin before studying the half page advert. He read, and as he read, he became more and more excited. He folded the paper, placed his wallet on top of it and rushed off to shower in preparation for a visit to the city.

Chapter Seven

Bad To The Bone

The following day, as the afternoon began to turn dusky, the night market was being set up in the square down to the left of Le Petit Lemon. The through road was closed by the gendarmerie as usual, stalls were erected and the small stage was cubed together under the market roof. Electrical cables were snaked and looped haphazardly across to a viper's nest of dangerous looking socket blocks that everyone seemed to tap into for their stalls, lighting, refrigerators and sound systems. Long trestle tables and the wooden benches from the school sports hall were trooped in by stall-holders to allow the expected throng to sit. As the evening fell the coloured lightbulb strings draped around the market's filigree ironwork were lit to enhance the subdued, natural illumination in the enclosed square. The logs in the boucherie's firepit were ignited. Cases of wine were ripped open and the chinking, crunching sound of bottles of wine being loaded into large plastic ice boxes melded with the warm spitting of the fire as the roasting meats dripped onto it, forcing awaiting mouths to salivate.

In the area surrounding the town, the setting, warm sun threw a glow over the responding sunflowers and man-high sweet corn fields. The regimented vines soaked the life-giving warmth and light, basking before the proper chill of the evening. The converging roads to the town were lost among this green wonderland. The farm workers had long since finished and the only sounds in the perfect blue skies were the distant screech of a pair of buzzards, circling high in the distance and the nearer coarse caws of the crows in a dense copse of oak trees; everywhere else was noiseless.

At this time one of the smaller landowners, on the plain below the town was sitting on his veranda, sipping a slightly coarse rosé, waiting for his wife to cook his evening meal after a day in the field. He was savouring the tang in his cheeks from the wine and these sights and sounds. His tuned ears then became aware of something else. A vehicle approaching possibly? No, this was something else. He asked in a gruff tone if his wife had the radio or TV on to spoil his repose, to which she curtly replied "Non!" Do you think your meal cooks itself, she thought.

The farmer stood from his cushioned rocking chair, still cupping his chilled wine; he was intrigued. The whirring sound grew nearer. it wasn't mechanical, was it? But yes, it must be! Then as if to confuse his thoughts even further—music! But what music? Suddenly, as sometimes happens with music and memories, the man was transported back to his heavy metal youth; his long lank hair; his denim jacket. What was that sound? Yes it was—mingled in the back of the electrical hum was a drum beat, but not just any drum beat, a heavy beat to one of his favourite songs. His head started nodding involuntarily to the beat as he heard 'Bad to the Bone' being hammered out across the summer air by George Thorogood and the Destroyers. The sound grew near and the man focussed on the fields to the left; he saw a shiny black dome whisking along the tops of the sunflowers following the line of the road. Then, passing, at what seemed like at least 40 kilometres per hour, was a man wearing mirrored aviator sunglasses, a white silk scarf wrapped across his face as if to enhance the mystique of the apparition. He was dressed in a black leather jacket with the black, half hat, crash helmet on his head and sat astride a silver steed, a powerful steed, a 750 watt electric cycle with chrome enhancements, good for 60 kilometres at a steady pace but with a top speed of 64 kilometres per hour if the throttle was wrung fully open. The strange rider passed with a hum, a glint of sunlight and was gone into the distance towards the town like some knight advancing on the awaiting battlements. The farmer stood with his mouth slightly agape; he had seen the man and seen the steed. The sound of the song lingered on the warm air and still continued as the mysterious rider faded into the distance. He poured another glass of wine from his carafe, raised his glass of rosé towards the rider and said quietly, "Salut!"

In the town the market was starting to hum with the sound of visitors as they flowed in and mingled among the stalls. In one corner of the square in an area with restricted parking sat two gleaming Harley Davidson motorcycles, drawing a crowd of boy admirers. None of them dared to touch, though, the owners of these low, fat, black hogs were sat outside Le Petit Lemon. Baz 'Bazzer' Arnot, president of the coastal outlaw motorcycle gang, the Bandidos, and his muscular sergeant-at-arms, known just as Hammer, had removed their 'patched' leather waistcoats, and were enjoying a cold beer and warming their numerous bulging tattoos in the dwindling evening sun. Both motorcycles were of the later generation 114 cubic inch engines, Bazzer favouring the raked forks, swirling blue paintwork and chrome of the breakout style chopper, while his lieutenant rode the aptly named, all black, Fat Boy. The two men were looking forward to a good meal and a few cold beers, before returning to the coast. They and the patrolling police had already given each other a mutually understanding nod that there would be no trouble this evening. All was at peace.

It would be wrong to say the peace was shattered but there was, for sure, a slight commotion over by the Harleys. Bazzer and Hammer immediately took notice from their seats in the sun. Humming in from an adjacent side street rode the mystery rider. He steered his own shiny steed confidently through some admiring spectators, into the tight space between the two much larger bikes and kicked his side stand down with a swagger that gave the impression he was a member of that same infamous biker gang. Then, rather than stepping through the gap where a fuel tank or cross-bar would usually be, he swung his leg over the back of the bike like he was in fact dismounting a stallion. Bazzer and Hammer looked from behind their wrap-around sunglasses with amazement, only their eyebrows giving away how wide their eyes were. Hammer tensed, rippled and went to get up. Bazzer just raised his hand slightly from the table in command. Hammer sat back into his seat obediently.

The mystery biker stood beside his machine and removed his helmet and the silk scarf from around his face. It was Gerald. Tucking his helmet under his arm, he nodded appreciatively at the machines next to his and as he stepped from between them patted the handlebars of Hammer's bike in a sign of biker kinship. Again Hammer rippled and got further up from his seat. This time Bazzer grabbed Hammer's inked forearm and levered him gently back into his seat. Gerald, oblivious to this potential threat to life, strode with a newfound confidence, that only a machine like his could give a man, over to Le Petit Lemon. As he approached the bar he noticed the two gentleman bikers at the table outside the bar. He stepped onto the pavement, dipped his sunglasses and saluted his *brothers* with two fingers to his forehead and a wide smile, before skipping into the bar. Bazzer felt Hammer's forearm tendons straining and noticed a small vein raised in his temple as he again tried to rise from the chair, but again Bazzer pulled him back into his seat.

Inside the bar Gerald was greeted by a gaggle of admirers and he began to explain all the intricate, technical specifications of his new found mode of transport, advising some of the, obviously jealous, members of the audience that he could probably get them a good deal on their own purchase if so inclined. Such was the interest and excitement that no-one appeared to notice the sound in the square of the joint angry roar of 3,120 cubic inches of Milwaukee's best iron loosening cobblestones as the Bandidos left their half drunk, cold beers and the square. Gerald was elated. The ride from the city in his new youthful 'biker' attire had been exhilarating and his friends' exuberance over his new bike made him feel like a new man. He hadn't felt this good about himself since...well, since before Annabelle.

Chapter Eight

Christina

That same evening the trestle benches of the market began to fill and with the warmth of the evening, the fair, the mediocre band and the people, it all collaborated to create one of those beautiful milieu that if someone new was subject to it, that someone would remember it always. As the evening light dwindled and the soft street lights pervaded, the square hummed with the chatter of happy people and cover songs and Gerald mingled and chatted with friends, old and new. On a number of occasions he would naturally rise from his seat to pull a chair out for a lady to sit down. Most did not even notice; to some, these gestures were just part of Gerald's strange *Englishness,* but to one onlooker it was the sign of a man, a gentleman. Christina Dubois had arrived in the Town that very day. She was visiting from Lyon with a view to buy and was staying with Madame LaFoy, who was a friend of a friend. Christina had visited the town in the past on holidays with her late husband and had always loved the area. Since the death of her husband, three years before, she had grieved and now believed a move would assist in that process. Consequently she had contacted Madame LaFoy and arranged to stay with her for two weeks to look at potential properties.

Christina is a petite, slender woman with a silvery bob of fine hair. She doesn't look her 66 years of age and like many French 'city' women is always immaculately and classically dressed. She had no intentions that evening other than to relax from the journey from Lyon and to soak up some of the soothing southern ambience and so she had accompanied Madame LaFoy to the market. But suddenly now, here was this man. She could tell without hearing his voice that he was an Englishman. It is a known fact that when any person takes time to people watch, humankind is adept at recognising certain body languages; just from Gerald's mannerisms, movements and facial expressions, Christina could tell. She had found herself unconsciously studying him. There was something, some element that reminded her of her perfect man, her dear husband. She became so focussed that she didn't even realise that Gerald had, as is also human nature, become aware that someone was observing him. He glanced once and then looked. In that moment both stared into each other's eyes. Those that have experienced this look would describe it as briefly becoming subject to tunnel vision, that all around slows and sound disappears. Then Christina smiled, a smile that Gerald, in time, would never forget. Christina felt herself blush slightly and she looked away and began talking to Madame LaFoy about something quite inconsequential. Gerald however continued to stare. That captivating look had been enchanting. He now studied this lovely woman a few benches away—the lines of her face, the movement of her mouth and her shining hair. Suddenly the spell was broken as Phillipe Renoir, the local immobilier agent leaned in across Christina's shoulder and Gerald's view and offered her his hand. Gerald couldn't hear what was being said but the woman had smiled warmly and when Renoir grasped her hand gently and touched it to his lips he felt a tinge of something deep down inside his gut.

Now Gerald had never really taken to Renoir. When he and Annabelle had first come to the town Gerald had spent a very uncomfortable two weeks of house hunting, where Renoir and Annabelle would inevitably end up sitting in the front of the estate agent's enviable Citroen SM while Gerald would sit in the back. All Renoir's attentive charms of house selling had been towards Annabelle, even though Gerald held the meagre purse strings. Renoir had, on a number of occasions, attempted to pry Annabelle away on individual viewings; he had even mooted a job for her within his agency. If Gerald were to describe Renoir he would have placed him somewhere between two acting legends, Terry Thomas and Hugh Grant in Brigitte Jones Diary (which he had been forced to watch too many times by Annabelle); in other words, an absolute cad and a bounder. That all said, Renoir had always been very pleasant to Gerald on the occasions when they had been on their own together. Gerald found that Renoir, as some people tended to, would encroach on Gerald's personal space. Renoir would also ask personal questions of Gerald that he found perplexing and uncomfortable, such as what perfume Gerald used. Renoir was also always attired beautifully and immaculately groomed, which again made Gerald feel slightly shabby when he was around him.

Gerald turned away and continued to converse with his surrounding friends, who had not noticed any of this fleeting emotional turmoil. Gerald continued to glance across occasionally, drawn to the elegance of this woman who he had never seen before. He tried to be inconspicuous but he twice noticed that she had made a sideways glance in his direction.

As the evening continued there was a conversation between Renoir and the woman where she and he rose from their seats, he kissed her on both cheeks and after a short further conversation flounced off in his pristine linen suit. Madame LaFoy rose also and said a few words to the woman, also kissed her on both cheeks and then left. The woman sat again, with an empty chair on either side of her. She sat and appeared to be listening attentively to the band's renditions of some old classics. Gerald felt like a boy again at his first school dance, watching a girl he liked standing against the other wall of the gym; letting the last dance end, not asking her to dance and knowing that the feeling of regret would accompany him home. But Gerald was not a boy anymore; there was no time in life left for feelings of regret. Gerald had never been a courageous man when it came to women. Other boys and men had always had the confidence and the witty chat-up lines. Gerald had met most of the women he had been in relationships with through long term associations at work. This evening would be different though. He felt confident, and also fortified by the two glasses of local red wine he had sipped during the evening, he began to weave his way over. As he did so he thought he noticed another half glance from the woman. But as he approached her, her gaze remained on the band; Gerald's confidence began to waver.

He cleared his throat.

"Excuse moi, madame?" he said.

Christina turned slowly; she knew the man had been approaching.

"Yes, monsieur," she responded softly in English, to set him at ease, as she had immediately realised from his accent that her assumptions were correct.

Gerald half smiled, also realising what the woman had done.

"May I sit with you? I mean... is anyone sitting here?" he said.

In perfect English she responded,

"Monsieur, to answer both of your questions, there is no-one sitting here now, and you are welcome to sit with me." Christina set the man at ease again.

Gerald knew again what the woman had done and felt warmed. Before he sat, and with a reinvigorated confidence, Gerald asked if the woman would like some wine and when she responded positively he had quickly fetched two glasses and a plastic carafe of a soft red wine from one of the vineyard stalls. He carefully poured the wine with as much decorum as the plastic container would allow. He had asked everything obvious without trying to make it sound like, 'Do you come here often?'

Christina could sense that Gerald was not at ease talking to women. She was happy that he was obviously not some charlatan and she kept the happy dialogue flowing. Gerald was oblivious to her womanly intuition and thought the conversation was going extremely well. As the evening waned they got to know each other and introduced themselves with their first names, although Gerald would never have been so presumptuous as to call her by it at this early stage. He had been openly excited by the fact that Christina was to be in the area for a number of weeks, although she had been careful not to offer why. During their conversations Christina was open and honest about the death of her husband. She told Gerald she had grieved and compartmentalised it and never thought discussing the matter was a burden to others. She had told Gerald this and explained that she had had thirty five wonderful years of faithful, happiness from a man who believed in living what life you have to the fullest degree.

Gerald looked at Christina and in a totally un-Gerald like manner said,

"Madame, you have wonderful eyes, but I can see still see there is some sadness in them."

Christina paused slightly and said intuitively,

"Of course, I miss the man. A loss like that scars your eyes with tears. But I can see there is also sadness in yours, Monsieur Gerald."

The crow's feet at the corners of her pale blue eyes crinkled as she smiled at Gerald knowingly. Gerald exhaled in a half laugh, caught red handed, like a simple man. Then they both laughed. Gerald raised his glass and Christina, hers. They chinked the durable glasses together. Then Gerald sighed and began to tell this woman, who he had just met, the thing he had spoken to no-one of; the story of Annabelle. They talked and confided and then laughed and were serious again and then laughed again. Their easy chatter flowed, Gerald did not even have time to consider how easy Christina was to talk to. Then, before they knew where time had gone, the slightly drunken announcer on the stage stated that the last dance was about to begin. Gerald looked at Christina and said.

"Do you know, for the longest time I haven't wanted to dance but tonight I feel very differently. Would you even dare to join me?"

Christina smiled and said

"Gerald, not only would I dare but I would actually enjoy that very much."

Gerald took her delicate, warm hand lightly and led her to the crowded dance area. He had not forgotten his middle aged lessons in dance and Christina fell into step as he led her in a waltz to the totally inappropriate song that was being played. As the evening ended Gerald asked Christina if he could escort her back to Madame LaFoy's townhouse, which he knew. He walked at a purposely slow pace to be able to continue their conversations about each other, shielding her from the odd noisy moped rider who passed them down the narrow but cosy streets. At Madame La Foy's residence Gerald opened the large, high, double wrought iron gates which gave a squeal as he walked Christina through to the path leading to the front door. At the step to the door Gerald stopped.

"Madame," he said, " I've had the most wonderful evening I've had for such a long time, without the assistance of too much wine."

Christina smiled,

"And I also, Gerald, but there's no need for wine when you are talking to me; and please call me Christina."

Gerald, who had smiled so much this evening, smiled once more.

"Goodnight Christina...umm...I would love to see you again,' Gerald said as a statement rather than a question.

"I am sure you will Gerald," she said in a heartfelt tone. There was an uncomfortable pause. He desperately wanted to kiss Christina's hand or her cheek but as always with shy men he missed the moment and took her hand and shook it gently. Then off he strode to the gates where he closed them behind him, pleased that she had waited at the door to wave to him as he did so. He sauntered home elated but with every footstep home, regretted that he hadn't kissed the woman.

Christina walked into the hallway of the townhouse, after waving Gerald goodnight, sighed with a smile and thought how glad she was that this lovely man had not tried to kiss her on the first occasion

Chapter Nine

The LoVe Bug

Gerald had worked for Domaine St Patrice for three and a half years now and the head vintner, Jules, had come to rely on Gerald for more than just labouring around the estate. Gerald had been keen to learn Jules' craft and although it did gnaw at Jules whether an Englishman would ever understand his skill with processing the grapes from the old vines into the soft wines, he actually liked Gerald and his enthusiasm to learn his trade. Gerald had slowly worked through each of the processes from the ground up, literally. The last three months Gerald had studied the blending of the lesser fruits and the refining of the better crops into the single strand wines that the Domaine cherished and laid down to age. Rather than quaffing the wine, Gerald had been taught the way to savour the wines that were ready: breathing in the vapours, checking how the wine hung to the side of the glass when whirled around it, sucking, slurping, washing around the mouth and spitting out—all the things that Gerald had always thought preposterous but now realised that every action was necessary and affiliated with the production of a fine wine. Jules would let Gerald complete parts of the operation without supervision and only check his work once completed. Gerald thoroughly enjoyed his new found skills; it made his employment so much more satisfying.

On one particular day Jules sent word and called Gerald to the vast cellars. Gerald made his way down the cool vaulted corridors past rows of barrels. The evenly spaced light bulbs hung and eerily pooled the light, enhancing the brick arches and alcoves. Jules waited as he had done numerous times before to test Gerald's knowledge. He had an upturned barrel with two crystal clear glasses perched on top of it and a small carafe of red wine. He stood under a single light hanging from a beam by a length of green fabric covered electrical flex. Gerald walked up to Jules in the lit environment

"You asked to see me Jules?" he asked.

"Qui Gerald. What do you think of this?" Jules said pouring the wine into the two glasses and handing Gerald one of them with a quarter inch of the deep red liquid sitting in the bottom of it. Gerald took the glass, carefully holding the stem near the base between his thumb and two fingers. Gerald remembered all Jules had taught him; he had been tested in a similar fashion many times before. Jules began his own tasting but continued to watch Gerald from above the rim of his own glass.

Gerald held the glass up to the light from the single light bulb, he gently swirled the liquid high up the inside of the glass. The plummy essence fell in drapes down the glass, pooling back in the bottom. He reviewed the fall of the wine that remained high in the glass, checking the colour and speed of the descent. Then he carefully drew the open top of the glass to his nostrils. It has to be said that Gerald had an ideal nose for the job; slightly large, sharp and straight, it slotted well into the void of the glass. He drew the fumes into his awaiting sensory channels and closed his eyes. His nostril hairs bristled excitedly; Gerald was always amazed how the smell was always slightly different every time. He logged in his mind how dense it was, and how many underlying aromas made up the complete bouquet. Then, still not uttering a word, he drew the rim of the glass to his lips and slowly and noisily drew in a sip to his mouth. The tang of the liquid burst against the inside of Gerald's cheeks and sent an aching sensation into the crux of his jawbone. Then the vanilla and peaches washed over his palate and tongue, changing immediately into a deeper flavour mildly reminiscent of summer pudding with blackberries and blackcurrants mingled with sweet, sticky suet.

Gerald further slurped some air through the little fluid and then collected it on top of his tongue and discourteously spat it into the shiny steel bucket on the floor beside the barrel.

"I'd happily drink that at Chez Michel, Jules," Gerald eventually said, continuing, "congratulations my friend, I believe you've done it again and produced a real winner." Jules smiled and looked at Gerald. He picked up the carafe and filled both their glasses with some more of the wine.

"I agree, Gerald," he said raising his glass to his colleague and friend. "I'd love to take the credit for this exquisite drink but this is yours, Gerald. We'll be laying this down under your name. The blend you have created and the depth of flavours are commendable."

Gerald just stared at Jules in the bright dome of light. He had a lump in his throat and he felt his eyes becoming watery.

"But how?" Gerald questioned.

Jules said, "Yes, I checked every step of the way from when the grapes were harvested but I didn't lay a hand on the process. You're quick to learn and you've already done so but will, in time, become a very fine vintner my friend. I have spoken to Madame Cecilly. She's tasted the wine and has agreed to promote you to vintner supervisor; you'll still work under me and will become my full-time assistant."

Jules could see the emotion in Gerald's face and stepped forward and put his hand on his shoulder.

"It is like your first child Gerald, eh!" Jules said with a smile. Gerald's face lit up around his weepy eyes and he smiled. Both men raised their glasses and drained Gerald's creation. Then Jules' demeanour changed slightly and he said,

"Madame Cecilly has said she will want to see you to confirm the promotion— apologies, my friend!"

Two days later on a bright sunny day, Gerald sat with his colleagues on one of the picnic benches situated on the grass verge at the top of one of the vine fields. All the men were taking their lunch break with their supplied lunch of home produced pate, local goats cheese and bread torn from fresh baguettes. A large carafe of pinot noir fulfilled their liquid refreshment requirements. The air was convivial. Gerald sat in discussion, slowly picking at his bread and cheese, the straps of his dungarees slung loosely about his waist and his feet in his chunky, one size too large, wellington boots were warm in the sun. The amiable, pastoral scene was disrupted by the distant, hushed whine of an electric motor; even the surrounding birdsong hushed at the sound. The men around the table knew it was too late to make a break for it and sat in silence with their heads bowed toward their food platters. The Vuitton buggy drew to a skid on the gravel drive beside the bench, sending a cloud of dust wafting along the road.

Mme Cecilly sat at the wheel in a pale blue, knitted trouser suit—a vintage 1970s Chanel ensemble. Her patent pale blue leather loafers had a film of dust covering them. She smiled thinly at the gathered employees and called in a light and airy greeting, "Bonjour messieurs!" The assembled collective knew better than to not respond and all hailed back at their employer with various waves of hands. Satisfied at the response, Mme Cecilly smiled brightly with her glossy maroon lips. Her powder blue eyelids crinkled as she did so.

"Monsieur Gerald, une moment, sil vous plait!" she called.

Gerald, although only sitting next to one colleague could swear he felt three of four pairs of hands pushing him from the sanctity of the bench. He quickly looped his dungaree straps over his shoulders, sloppily extracted his wellies from under the bench and walked towards the gaudy, waiting vehicle. As he approached, the driver's side of the buggy, Mme Cecilly slid across the bench seat to the passenger side and patted the warm driver's seat with her immaculately manicured and red painted fingertips, beckoning Gerald to take up the driver's position.

Now, Gerald had, on occasions, driven the 'Love Bug', as it had become affectionately known by the men at the vineyard, but only on his own. The buggy had a simple forward and reverse shift stick in the dashboard panel and two pedals on the floor, a large brake pedal and a smaller 'go' pedal just to the right of it. Gerald sat as requested, but as close to the edge of the seat as he possibly could without falling out of the buggy.

"Bonjour Madame!" he politely said.

Mme Cecilly tapped the windscreen upright with her, up until now, hidden riding crop and ushered Gerald forward with her free left hand. "Allez, allez, Gerald!" she said, smiling. Gerald selected drive and awkwardly but tentatively pressed the accelerator with his large boot. The buggy slid forward smoothly up the mile-long gravel trackway. He didn't see his relieved compatriots waving happily to him and raising their glasses as he pulled away up the driveway.

As the buggy pulled out of earshot of the other workers Mme Cecilly half turned towards Gerald. She reverted to her perfect English and in an out of character, friendly manner said,

"Gerald, you are probably aware that I have spoken to Jules about your employment here at Domaine St Patrice. He has informed me of your excellent work ethic and self-generated enthusiasm for learning. I have sampled your Cuvee and although not quite up to Jules' standard yet, it was a very palatable mix." Gerald found himself smiling and said, "Thank you, Madame!"

Mme Cecilly continued and in a lapse from her confident English tongue stated, "It has been agreed that you will, how would you say, become the apprentice to Jules. There will be some small increase in your wage; *small,* I would reiterate!" Mme Cecilly, like her father before her was not known for her generosity when it came to her employees' wages.

Gerald continued to smile in a relaxed manner and again repeated,

"Thank you, Madame!" Mme Cecilly also seemed to relax at completing any formal discussion with Gerald and said,

"And now we shall enjoy the drive, Gerald"

This was a statement rather than a question, Gerald felt. Mme Cecilly looped the strap of her crop over her slender right wrist and reached in to the inside pocket of her jacket and retrieved a well-worn, leather-bound, antique, glass drinks flask. She expertly removed the silver topped cork and said to Gerald,

"We should drink now to confirm your appointment!" She held the flask up to Gerald's mouth.

Gerald managed to utter,

"Madame, I don't think I should as I'm driv..." before Mme Cecilly pressed the smooth glass rim of the flask into Gerald's parted lips and half-filled his mouth with the warm sweet Calvados the flask contained. She pulled the flask free and raised it to her own mouth and took a healthy swig. This set Gerald's mind partly at ease, that Cecilly had taken a drink from the same flask. He swallowed what was in his mouth. As smooth as it was it burned his throat, then his chest and eventually sent a hot flow into his non-consenting stomach. The hot, dusky apple scent flowed around his still burning cheeks as he finally exhaled the hot fumes from his lungs.

"That's better! We're relaxing now!" Mme Cecilly said quietly. Gerald stared dead ahead and maintained a steady speed, hoping to find a turning point for the buggy. The track, although well-trodden with road chippings, had some indiscernible dips and bumps in its surface. Consequently the buggy did rise and fall and bump on its non-existent suspension. Gerald heard Mme Cecilly mutter, "Oh these roads, so unsteady!" She looked out to her right as if nonchalantly surveying the vines and at the same time rested her bony left hand lightly on Gerald's right knee, as if steadying her frail self. Gerald gripped the gold, leather-wrapped steering wheel tighter with both hands and continued to stare straight ahead.

The driveway they were following was one of many that dissected and surrounded the estate; covering miles in length they formed a lattice of routes for maintaining the hundreds of acres of ancient vines. If unaware of the specific topography of the estate one could drive these roads for hours without seeing a soul. As their journey continued Gerald became more and more concerned that he was driving in to oblivion. This concern began to rise on a sliding scale as Mme Cecilly took another couple of swigs from her flask. The bumps in the road had a two-fold effect. Firstly, as Mme Cecilly drank from the flask a bump in the road would jolt more Calvados into her mouth. Secondly, and more concerning to Gerald, at each coinciding bump Mme Cecilly's hand would move further up Gerald's leg by an inch or so, to steady herself.

Eventually this coincidental sequence of events took a worrying turn for both the occupants of the vehicle. A particularly large divot in the road that Gerald could not avoid caused a larger than expected mouthful of Calvados in Mme Cecilly's mouth and her hand slipped to within three inches of Gerald's crotch. Now Gerald could in all honesty have dealt with this uncomfortable situation but the larger than usual mouthful of Calvados in Mme Cecilly's mouth, and the burning in her cheeks and throat, caused such a distraction that she neglected to control the strength of her grip on Gerald's nether region. To Gerald, as he briefly looked down at his upper thigh, he envisioned a surreal Eagle's claw gripping his thigh. The bones, sinew and red talons came together in a vice-like grip that caused one last ruinous consequence; Gerald's right leg unconsciously straightened like a steel rod. This forced the accelerator to the floor and jammed his wellington boot under the lip of the brake pedal. Retraction was impossible, as much as Gerald tried. His foot wallowed about in the large boot, unable to get any purchase to pull and release it from the mechanical hold. The uprated Louis Vuitton cart immediately shot forward and instantly accelerated to its maximum speed of 28 miles per hour.

The buggy sped up the gravel track billowing clouds of dust behind it. Mme Cecilly grasping the A pillar of the windscreen and Gerald's high, inner thigh let out a 'Whoop!' thinking that Gerald was trying to make the drive more exciting for her. Gerald, in contrast was done with excitement and his mind whirled for an answer to the predicament. He knew the buggy would probably get to Marseille before it ran out of charge. Unfortunately for Gerald, he was aware that the on-off switch had been disabled by the estate mechanic at Mme Cecilly's direction because of the number of keys she had lost over the years, so in effect the buggy was constantly live. His thought processes also had to deal with the rivulets of pain searing through his thigh and groin as Mme Cecilly's grip did not subside but with the increased speed, if anything, tightened. In that moment it came to him—the balance ponds!

The ponds were dotted across the estate. They were excavated and landscaped in strategic locations and served multiple purposes. In times of rainfall, which at times could be torrential, the ponds captured the flow of water down their natural courses and by capturing the flow, slowed it all to a manageable out-flow that stopped flooding and soil wash. They also formed important reservoirs to supplement the estate's water supplies and were good natural habitats for the local flora and fauna. Gerald knew there was a pond some half a mile further up the track. If he could just lock out the pain and traverse the grassy slopes to the water it would provide the ultimate brake.

Mme Cecilly was oblivious to Gerald's consternation, in fact she was enjoying the wind in her wispy hair and the feeling of speed as the vines sped past and a man's muscular thigh in her hand. The buggy broke out of the vines up the grey track into the open. Gerald saw the grassed area on the left with the sunken rectangular pond some three hundred metres away. He wrenched the steering wheel to the left and jolted up onto the short cut grassed area. He set a course for the pond. Mme Cecilly, in her happy state, only took a few seconds to work out that there was obviously a problem. She looked at the floor and saw the issue with the accelerator. She tried pulling Gerald's leg back with her fingers digging deeper to no avail. She briefly looked at Gerald who appeared to be smiling like a demon at her, but was in fact grimacing in pain with the increased clench, pain like he'd never felt before. Mme Cecilly also worked out Gerald's answer to the problem as she saw the pond. All of these realisations took place in a split second. Mme Cecilly's next thought was, bizarrely, Chanel. Her suit! And much as she felt she should support Gerald, the suit was dry clean only. She saw her opportunity as a large pile of fresh cut vine shoots and hay had been piled just ahead on her side of the buggy. She grasped the A frame and releasing her grip on Gerald's thigh she leaped from the buggy. Remembering her parachute training from earlier life, she executed a perfect knee bend, tuck and roll, bowling at high speed into the pile and disappearing in a puff of pale blue and green.

The resultant release of his upper thigh sent a wave of ecstatic relief through Gerald's appreciative body and mind. Nothing that was about to befall him from the impending impact with the pond mattered any more. It was too late to bail out now. Gerald braced. The buggy breached the top of the slope that led down to the water and took off. Gerald screamed. The vehicle briefly touched down for a split second before it nosedived into the still waters. Gerald thought the steering wheel was going to break as it bowed in to an oval shape under his straight arm clench. The resultant splash and opposing force of the water immediately slowed the little buggy but it continued to drive forward under the surface. Within moments Gerald found himself up to his neck in pond. He heard the electric motor click and die. He took a breath as the little brown and gold roof disappeared beneath the resultant tsunami. Gerald released his hold on the wheel and using his free hands pulled his trapped leg free from the still wedged boot. Kicking his other wellington boot off he pulled himself free from the side of the buggy and surfaced exhaling and drawing fresh breath.

Back in the cuttings Mme Cecilly's face peered from the pile. She grimaced as she saw her beloved buggy and the straining neck and head of Gerald disappear beneath the surface. She extracted herself from the soft clippings and hay. She brushed herself down and removing the hip flask from her pocket, which had miraculously survived, she took a swig to steady her nerve and set off to find some staff to arrange recovery of the buggy. Gerald surfaced in time to see Mme Cecilly sauntering off with a purpose, swigging from her flask. He felt no bitterness toward the dotty old dame; in fact, he was relieved she was OK and making her way back to the vinery. He began to swim for the grass bank.

Later that day, Gerald got his bedraggled self back to the main cellars and sought out Jules. Jules already knew about the buggy because Mme Cecilly had instructed him to arrange recovery from the pond with no explanation as to Gerald's whereabouts, or how the buggy had become ensconced in the pond. Jules explained that Mme Cecilly had agreed Gerald's promotion and signed the necessary paperwork. They sat in the warm afternoon sun and shared a plastic tub of warm rosé , Jules laughing loudly as Gerald recounted the adventure and showed him the perfect claw impression on his upper thigh. Both men sat drinking into the evening and as the Love Buggy came past on the back of the low loader still weeping pond water, and with Gerald's wellington still firmly fixed on the accelerator, they both laughed and looked to lock up Domaine St Patrice for the night.

Chapter Ten

La Plage

On the back wall of the bar in Le Petit Lemon hangs a calendar, a yearly gift from the local wine producers to whom Hugo was ever grateful. The month of July had just been turned over to show a pretty woman with an ample bosom, in a crisp white dress wandering through a field of lavender, holding a large glass of the local rosé. Significantly though, a pin with a small flag had been thrust into a date at the end of the month. On the flag was written 'La Plage'. Every year, just prior to the French national holidays in August Hugo and the invited patrons of Le Petit Lemon would organise a trip to the beach. It was an affair that all but the wives of the patrons looked forward to. Gerald, when first a resident of the town, was not invited for the first year's venture; he had not then served sufficient time as a customer and could not understand where all of his new found friends had disappeared to on that long, hot July day. But for this, and the past three years, he had received the invite and now clearly understood what all the excitement was about; the trips to the beach were the stuff of legend.

Hugo was the director and main organiser; to him it was his two weeks holiday rolled into eighteen hours, consequently, woe betide any person who saw fit to disrupt, disagree or contradict his plans. Hugo's cousin, Alfonse, who ran a local taxi company, supplied the transport for the venture. The small coach, which dated from 1959, was a classic Setra 10 series, model 6, that Alfonse had restored some years ago. Alfonse would show the coach at many of the local vintage car shows. Now resplendent in cream and pale blue coachwork, the shining grill and chrome Bezel headlights gave the small bus an amiable face. The swirling paintwork was highlighted by long strips of chrome. The chrome and colour matched the hubcaps and the translucent blue, curved glass, skylight panels oozed art deco travel. It harked back to an era when these workhorses were not just built, but crafted with style, to convey passengers to different lands on quieter roads in luxury. In the past, this glorious charabanc had explored most of Europe but now she was used every year to convey the invited guests the 55 kilometres to a small beach at Cap d'Agde.

The menu for the day was drawn up personally by Hugo and distributed to various, trusted patron's wives, although Hugo always prepared the entree; he was not going to have his perfect day tainted by any potentially inept culinary skills from the chosen women. For those not already aware Hugo was, as the old saying goes, a confirmed bachelor, always had been and always would be. This was undoubtedly why there was a kinship between Hugo and all the male regulars at the bar who had never married or had once been, but were now single; this obviously included Gerald. A kinship that had been forged over the span of years and the large, hardwood bar.

The day approached and Hugo's preparations drew to a close and to his satisfaction. substantial quantities of alcohol were loaded onto the coach; accordingly, some years prior Alfonse had had the suspension uprated after an unfortunate incident with a cracked wishbone spring due to overloading. Fortunately for Alfonse it had not disrupted his cousin's day. The menu accompaniments that Hugo had ordered from the chosen wives in the town had been delivered and scrutinised thoroughly by him. In truth, the poor women dreaded the yearly dictate; their unsteady husbands would return from the bar proudly holding aloft the handwritten note from Hugo of what cuisine was required. They hated the weeks of preparation and self-testing of their small part of the feast. They all knew from previous experience what would happen if they got it wrong. The last wife who had, had found her delicate fish mousse with a fine cucumber and dill decoration, dumped unceremoniously into a cardboard box at the side of the bar beside the wheelie bins. Her husband had been castigated and ignored by Hugo at the bar for weeks after, and the consequent vicarious malice had been transferred to the home arena where the unfortunate woman had suffered miserably at the hands of her distraught husband until Hugo deigned to recognise him again. Fortunately most of the annual, quivering crowd of women who saw the bus off, got it right and a huge sigh of relief always flowed from them as one as they waved their loved ones *Bon voyage* for the day.

As the bus prepared to leave Gerald sat in the window seat and with a slight, unconscious glance noticed Phillipe Renoir's classic, gleaming, gold Citroen SM parked in the bright sunshine near his estate agency. The car from the 1970s was a classic car by all measures. Developed during Citroen's ownership of the Maserati marque in the late 1960s it was a car way ahead of its time, technically. From the smooth V6 Maserati engine to the encased headlights that followed the angle of the steering and the hydraulic suspension that even Rolls Royce took note of, the sleek Opron design was still modern by current standards. Phillipe had bought the car because he had loved the style, the design and the aura the car emitted. He justified the price the car cost five years ago by stating to himself, quite rightly, that the business and his own standing would benefit from such a classic and individual mode of transport. Renoir was standing beside the passenger side of the car in a crisp, pale blue suit, smirking as he opened the passenger door courteously for a smiling, perfect-looking Christina. After closing her door Renoir, clearly happy, skipped and trotted around the rear of the car and entered the driver's side. As the car started with its quiet V6 burble it slowly raised itself up on its air suspension. The rear lights flickered as Renoir selected drive and the large rear windscreen glinted in the sunlight as the beautiful car slid away up the street. Gerald's stomach churned and elation turned in a split second to misery, and his heart ached in his bony chest.

In contrast, at the front of the bus a very happy Hugo had, in his view, this year outdone himself. The volunteer chefs had produced more than passable dishes to accompany his *piece de resistance*, a whole 16 kilo salmon which had been poached to perfection with skewers of whole marinated garlic cloves and a chilled, piquant, poivron and chilli sauce to complement. He had laid it all on a bed of ice that morning in a substantial copper fish kettle, *borrowed* (given over under some duress) from the nearby Michelin starred 'Chez Michel'. Trestle tables and chequered covers were stowed below with the large parasols which had been poked into all the available crevices. Finally the exuberant, invited entourage had filed aboard and the ageing bus, under this massive combined weight, let out an animal groan from its gearbox and heaved itself forward. Hugo, had dressed for the occasion; newcomers were unused to seeing him out of his dirty apron. He wore a pale blue, dress shirt with frills down the button line, and open at the neck where he had tied a large patterned silk cravat. His substantial trousers were being upheld, under some strain, by a wide set of braces. Visually, he could well have been the celebrity tenor on his way to the opera house. He was seated right behind his cousin Alfonse, who was coaxing his old steed down the road. Hugo had the luxury of being the only one with a double seat to himself. All the other passengers had been allocated seats in tiers of current preference and favour. Gerald, still in some emotional turmoil did, however, feel very privileged to be only three rows from the front. Hugo was still chuckling every now and then about the notorious cycling shorts. He opened the only freezer box beside him, which had not been meticulously packed in the storage compartments below. He withdrew a large salver and began to stack the chilled creme de menthe ice lollies that had been set on silver sticks the night before. He passed one to Alfonse, who began to lick it appreciatively while deftly steering the coach's unpowered steering with one hand. Then Hugo began walking back down the aisle of the coach, almost doing a tango so as not to wedge himself between the seats while still keeping the tray balanced. There was much 'mmming' and 'cooing' as the strong, emerald green treats were distributed. Hugo eventually side-stepped his way back to the front of the coach and sat with his three remaining treats, he tasted the first mouthful but already knew they were good. Then he sat back to enjoy the perfect start to what he knew would be the perfect day.

Some two hours later, at Cap d'Agde, Alfonse found a spot in the free car park close to the beach and filled a row of parking spaces to place his old vehicular friend under the shade of the bordering trees to cool her down from the journey. The spot was a mere stone's throw from the expansive, soft sands of Le Richelieu Plage that led down to the cooling waters of the Mediterranean Sea. There was still work to be done however and the party had been, from experience, careful not to imbibe too much en route. Tables were carted and assembled, cloths spread, parasols erected and weighted and folding chairs clicked open and set about. The early wisps of cloud burnt off and the sun began to toast the sand, the sea shimmered and the stubby date palms moved gently in the Mistral's light breath.

Most of the gathering were already wearing their shorts and were pre-pared when they stripped off their vests, displaying the white 50 factor sun cream their worried wives had rubbed onto their bodies before they left. Gerald changed on the bus and having previously reviewed the latest beach fashions in the barber's collection of magazines, exited the bus wearing a very modern pair of knee length surfer shorts, which were pale blue, dotted with large white flowers. Following the latest craze further, Gerald had left his underwear on under the shorts and above the top of the shorts he had pulled the waistband of his boxer shorts up, displaying the words E LECLERC continuously emblazoned around them; after all Calvin Klein and G Star Raw were so very expensive. He ran across the small bordering dune and joined the friendly throng around the encampment.

Some five minutes later Hugo crested the dune from the bus. Now, those who had been before were aware of this sight, but those who hadn't stood open mouthed and their reactions were watched by those who had, with suppressed amusement. Hugo strode down through a wavering heat haze, across the sand to the co-joined tables. He carried a towel and wore nothing but a very small pair of black, men's, bikini briefs, which were totally lost from sight beneath his large, overhanging belly. His belly was in proportion, though, to his massive barrel chest, shoulders and back. He was covered from head to foot in thick, black curly hair, which could probably be attributed to some long-lost Greek ancestor. Across his chest and around his back a large band of hair had turned silvery grey with age. Consequently, from behind he had the stature and colouring of a male mountain gorilla from the Congo. His colossal build and colouring were further emphasised by the fact that after slipping into his trunks Hugo had sprayed his whole body with an aerosol can of good quality olive oil. Hugo had no need for SPF protection on his one day of the year in the sun. He advanced into camp and expressed his satisfaction at the configuration of the camp (which was exactly the same as last year). The first ice boxes were collected from the bus and apéritifs, small crudities and dips were consumed. The day had begun beautifully and all were in a carefree mood.

As the day warmed and flowed the beach began to get familial groups and canoodling couples dotted across it. Few of Le Petit Lemon's gathering noticed the slow encroachment to their peripheral area by a group of youths who had been arriving like flotsam on an incoming tide. They gathered as tribal clans do, saluting each other, as they arrived, with much fist touching and swaggering. As the sun touched its apex they numbered nearly twenty. They had created their own reservation and then the posse drum beat of a deep bass from the very large *boom box* began to reverberate across the hot sands. Bony bodied adolescents in impossibly baggy shorts and oversize baseball caps and sunglasses began strutting, gyrating, standing with arms folded and pointing two finger's downwards. Hugo and his party, although slightly perplexed, carried on and appeared unconcerned about the ethnic gathering next to their cultured occasion—after all *vivre et laisser vivre.*

Then, as if to test the patience of Le Petit Lemon's family, a balloon like beach football appeared and an impromptu match between the gathered youths began. Families and couples ducked for cover, to the amusement of the sand hoofing players, as the light ball was kicked and thrown with complete abandon. Twice the ball landed near to Hugo's resplendent banquet, with some tutting from his companions and no apology from the retrieving beach vermin. At some point, some would remember at different stages, the ball was launched into the air from an impressive aerial scissor kick to raucous cheers from the opposing teams. It soared high into a gentle arc and then fell...fell towards the uncovered salmon kettle. In a split second Hugo snatched up the sharp carving fork from the table and, in a musketeer style parry, thrust forward across the table and pierced the descending orb with a loud 'pop!' In the following few seconds that it took for the ball to stop hissing, the music machine had been switched off and eighteen young warriors, chests puffed out and shoulders strutting as if dancing to Status Quo, advanced on the confederacy of Le Petit Lemon. Hugo threw down the fork with the slightly gasping ball still attached to it and circumvented the table to meet the advancing horde.

And so it was that hot day; in the centre, Hugo's immense frame glistening in the bright, light backed by the fourteen men of the bar and Alfonse. Gerald would later admit he was nervous but still had some inner anger from the sight of Christina with Renoir earlier that day. He had never been involved in any form of conflict such as this; his inner anger was heightened, however, when one of the opposing youths spotted his underpants waistband, pointed it out to the others and began to laugh uproariously. The leader of the young men, however, was having none of the merriment and began pointing, his two fingers sideways with a cocked thumb and rapping his remonstrations. Hugo stood feet apart and hands on hips guarding his beloved and awaiting banquet. He sneered. He had often chased the similar local youths from the front of his bar, hating their rear facing hats, street spitting, aggressive, pseudo poet, graffiti spraying, totally un-French-like behaviour. He bothered to listen for a few moments to the boy's threats and then said, "Qui, mademoiselle?" The opposing group's eyes widened and, if it was possible, their chests puffed out even further and with fists clenched they ran at Hugo across the twenty metres that separated them. Hugo moved towards their advance followed by his loyal comrades.

The ancient sea fort that sat in the bay had not seen such a coming together for centuries. The two forces clashed together with a slap of oily bodies, the boy who unfortunately reached Hugo first flew into the air in a backward somersault having run into a fortress like forearm smash, and so the battle began. As the two groups advanced and young and old engaged in mortal combat, Alfonse sped off in the direction of the bus. Now, some initially thought him a coward; however, he was much slighter of frame than his cousin, having come from his grandfather's side—he required an advantage. Opening and dashing in through the door of the old bus he retrieved an oversized 'G' shape wheel brace, which he conveniently kept under the driver's seat. He set off back to the fray. Breaching the dune like a reinforcing cavalry unit, he drove onto the clamouring mass of overweight and underweight that were locked in individual tussles. The first youth he caught with a sideswipe of mildly warm steel across the left ear, sending the hapless boy sprawling in the sand and spilling the contents of his rucksack, six large aerosol cans of car spray paint accumulated for later street artwork. Alfonse advanced further into the melee stooping in an acrobatic manner to gather one of the cans of rather fetching blue paint. He advanced as his cousin's musketeer brother. He barred two flailing arms that came his way from two of the lads that confronted him, with the wheel brace. While the youths reeled in agony, Alfonse caught both full on with a broad and deep spray of the blue paint across their faces, up their noses and in their mouths. Screaming in an un-manlike fashion, clutching their eyes and throats they both lurched toward the sea like some extras in the film, Braveheart.

The young leader who Hugo had insulted, and his two lieutenants, decided to take out the opposing leader. They ran at Hugo. Two of them leaped and tried to wrap themselves around Hugo's tree-like arms and neck. The third went in for a tactical rugby tackle on his thighs, trying to down this monolith and deliver the coup d'etat. They were not, however, prepared for the good quality olive oil. In a move that any Grecko-style wrestler would have been proud of Hugo soon had the two upper offenders in a head-lock under each arm and the third, similarly head-locked between his thighs. In that position, Hugo fell to the sand on purpose, like some gangly alien tree, gripping all three tightly. Gerald was not in such a fortunate position. He himself was in the grip of a headlock from one of the larger protagonists and now sported a newly formed swelling to his left eye from an earlier wayward *haymaker*. As Gerald looked across from his enforced position he looked into the face of the doomed lad whose head was securely locked between Hugo's thighs. The boy was gagging and choking on a mass of thick black hair and flesh which smelt like his mother's larder. His ears had been forced forward and stuck out, his eyes bulged and his tongue was extended fully from his mouth. Bizarrely, in that split second, Gerald thought he looked like a gargoyle on a cathedral parapet. The lad's evil tongue was only one centimetre from the two, large, truffle shaped bulges wrapped in Hugo's sharkskin briefs that were his testicles. The first fortunate thing for this unfortunate rapper was that his tongue physically could not reach Hugo's testes, for if it had, the consequent, involuntary twitch would have undoubtedly broken the young man's neck like a dry twig. The second fortunate thing for the youth was that such was Hugo's strength and hold that within thirty seconds the lad had been rendered unconscious from his living, hairy hell. His two similarly unfortunate colleagues were both also rendered unconscious and relieved from sucking copious mouthfuls of sweat from each of Hugo's oily armpits.

In a clearing just beyond Hugo's spider like image of writhing limbs stood Jacques in a strong martial arts stance with his right leg bent at the knee and his left straight behind him, his hands and arms, to those who recognised it, moving from the Tiger to the Praying Mantis position. His eyes as usual not blinking as his head switched from side to side altering his peripheral vision. Beneath this triangular stance stood De Gaulle in a similar but four legged stance with his small white, pin like teeth and red gums bared. It was as if there was a forcefield surrounding them; a three metre circle in the sand with Jacques in the centre going through a ritual kata. No-one entered the circle and Jacques didn't move from the centre of it. Within the circle was serenity while all around the rumpus continued. It could be construed that no-one noticed Jacques, maybe the ancient Eastern teachings had allowed him to cast some mystical spell to become invisible, but most likely the sight of this slight but frighteningly starey-eyed figure and his dog was enough to keep friends and foes a sensible distance away. As Gerald surveyed the scene he was impervious to the pounding fists of his captor, he certainly wasn't aware of Alfonse dancing up behind his tormentor, driving the thick, crooked brace between the youth's legs and withdrawing it at speed catching the boy's man-tackle heavily with the crooked rapier. The vanquished lad had no further thought for Gerald and relinquished his hold of him, concentrating instead on grabbing the future of his family. In the time it took the significant pain to register with the youth, Alfonse had pirouetted around him and lunged in a perfect fencing move spraying the remnants of the blue aerosol paint into the lad's open and inhaling mouth. He toppled, gurgling blue bubbles.

Alfonse leant a supporting shoulder to Gerald and both watched as Hugo rose from the sand with his three vanquished foes about his hairy feet; Hugo let out a bullish bellow and beat his massive chest as if imitating his animal counterpart. Those youths who had not already been dispatched saw their battered leader face down in the sand, they scurried and dragged themselves back to their camp and belongings and then retreated further across the hot, sandy plain, their recovered beach towels waving, raggedly in the breeze like the colours of a defeated army. Hugo looked about himself and surveyed the withdrawing adversaries; he looked with pride at his valiant, bedraggled and bruised comrades, raised his mighty arm and shouted after the defeated, "Vive La France!'" All those around him and those spectators who had not left the beach and were lucky enough to have witnessed the spectacle shouted in echo, "Vive La France!" Then the band of victorious warriors recovered chunky jewellery, baseball caps, ear piercings and many inappropriate photos of the still unconscious foes. They returned to their well-defended and intact tables of food and set about the feast in an un-warrior like and well-mannered fashion.

As the sun began to set later that day and after the substantial, extensive and beautiful food, and much quaffing of good wines and spirits, the contingent, some still wearing their backward facing caps like trophies of war, re-loaded the small bus and set off for their sweet beckoning home. Hugo robed in a large pink beach towel settled himself into the two front seats behind his newly favoured cousin and pulled the cork from a particularly good bottle of Calvados with his teeth to complete, what had definitely been, the best holy-day ever.

When the coach eventually pulled into the softly-lit square outside Le Petit Lemon with a gentle squeal of brakes all was silent on board. His fatigued knights then man-handled and carried the now comatose King Hugo, as pallbearers would, at shoulder height from the coach, through the bar and laid him gently to rest on the large leather sofa in the back room. They ceremonially covered him with a soft blanket, then left, locking up the bar and putting the key back through the letterbox. Slowly the brave few dwindled into the dim side streets of the night, some alone, some with others still reminiscing about their day of glory. They swaggered back to their adoring womenfolk, who were woken and regaled with tales of derring-do. Those men that were still able and filled with the sap of battle also *treated* their surprised spouses to one final heroic exertion, which in all probability meant that spring would see an unexpected baby boom in the small town.

Gerald, having assisted his compadres in laying the king to rest, sauntered his weary, aching and bruised way back to his apartment. Still brimming with testosterone, the euphoria of victory and blinking out of his heavily swollen and black right eye, he had but one thing on his mind—another battle to be fought. He undressed in his apartment and laid prostrate on his back on his bed. He slowly lowered the packet of frozen peas on to the right side of his face and visualised his adversary—Phillipe Renoir.

Chapter Eleven

A Right French Farce!

One particular morning Gerald was up well before the 7am alarm from Henri; he had laid awake in bed from 5.30am, unable to contain his excitement at the fact that he would have Christina for the whole day to himself, showing her around a number of properties that he knew were for sale in the area. He'd been up and, in his naked attire, had over-tidied the apartment in anticipation of the fact she might come in for a while. He had set a coffee pot percolating noisily in the kitchenette which was filling the air with a warming aroma as he saw to his toilet and showered; he was pleased his swollen eye had reduced somewhat. At 7.45am the door to the apartment rattled to a soft knocking; Christina was early! Gerald wondered how she had bypassed the exterior door but assumed that Mme Joella had been close by and let her in. Gerald briefly paused at the mirror to check his look and hurried to the door. He opened it with a wide smile, a smile that allowed his jaw to drop open without muscular assistance as he was greeted by Mme Joella and standing behind her, a tearful, Annabelle. Annabelle brushed past Mme Joella in a whirl and, rolling her wheelie suitcase into the room past Gerald, threw her arms around his stiff, aching neck, exclaiming,

"Gerry, Oh! Gerry! Thank goodness!" Gerald stood transfixed only able to discern Mme Joella reaching in to grab the door handle to pull it closed with the only emotion showing on her face as she stared at him, an overtly raised left eyebrow.

It was a full fifteen seconds before Gerald's hearing and sense of feeling returned slightly and he perceived Annabelle's arms wrapped around his neck, her tears wetting his shirt, her lips brushing the odd kiss on his neck and the babbling white noise as she explained how frightened she had been that he would be gone and how the last two years without him had been hell, how she had made such a juvenile mistake by running off with Gianni, how he had never been mature enough for her and how she had fully realised that when he had started giving private tennis lessons to the wealthy daughter of a local vineyard owner, and how she should have realised that no good would come of it. Gerald, still dumbfounded, bizarrely, managed to recall, ironically, that that was how Annabelle had met and run off with Gianni originally, and how Gerald had scrimped and scraped to pay for her tennis lessons because she appeared so passionate about the game. Unfortunately it was not just the tennis she had been passionate about. The last time he had seen Annabelle she had been around him in exactly the same position and he had been in exactly the same stupor as she explained that Gianni was everything that she had ever wanted; he was who she was meant to be with and that she had made a terrible mistake and could he ever forgive her. He recalled he was still suffering some form of out-of-body experience as she dragged her wheelie case out to the waiting Gianni in his convertible Alfa Romeo, and seeing her sympathetically smiling face as she waved back to him, blowing him kisses when they left. He had been drunk for two weeks solidly afterwards; it was only the latent concerns of his now comrades at Le Petit Lemon that eventually weaned him to a lesser amount of alcohol, that had undoubtedly saved his life.

"Gerry, Gerry!" Annabelle's dulcet tone broke into Gerald's painful reminiscing. With womanly intuition Annabelle realised what Gerald was thinking and unlatched from his neck, she whirled around the apartment cooing and exclaiming how wonderful 'Gerry' had made the place look. Gerald hated the fact she called him Gerry—no-one else called him that and although he had told Annabelle this on a number of occasions during their brief relationship she seemed to revel in the fact that he allowed her to do it even though she knew he hated it.

"Oh! Your eye, Gerry darling," and "Ooh! That coffee smells so good!" she exclaimed. "Do you remember how I like it, you darling man?'"

Gerald unconsciously went like an automaton into the kitchen and poured Annabelle a cup of the black coffee with brown sugar, just the way she liked it. She sat on the settee in her short flowery dress and cupped her hands around the steaming brew, her blonde tresses curling at the sides in the steam. She stared into the black swirling liquid and without looking up said,

"Gerry, there's so much to say, so much to put right, we need to get back to those happy summer, halcyon days we had. He left me with an empty heart and an empty bank account. I know now what a waste of life it's been for me being away from you. I need to mend all that hurt."

Gerald sat on the edge of the chair opposite Annabelle still trying to gather his thoughts in amongst the utterly incredulous feeling that he was back where he was five years ago, with no thoughts of his own, his life being steered, manipulated, railroaded. He looked at her and he saw what he had always loved physically and loathed mentally. It was like a spell—he was powerless. His hands tingled with pins and needles and he realised he wasn't breathing as he listened to her inane, simpering but assertive tones.

Gerald had lost all sense of time, of his surroundings, of his mind. The door reverberated to the same knock as thirty minutes ago; was this deja vu, he thought? No, Annabelle was still sitting in front of him, her continuous chatter halted only by the knock at the door. Gerald shook his head and averted his stare from Annabelle, got up and walked unsteadily to the door. He opened it and Mme Joella stood there exactly as before but this time standing behind her was Christina, smiling and looking classically beautiful in a pale blue summer dress. For a second no-one spoke, Gerald stared at Mme Joella, who, if it was possible, raised her eyebrow even further towards her hairline. Christina broke the silence and said

"Monsieur Gerald?" with the softest smile.

Before Gerald could respond, even with a smile he felt Annabelle draped on his shoulder.

"Oh Gerry, how inconsiderate of me, I should have known you could never keep this place as clean as this on your own; is this your lovely cleaning lady? Hello, I'm Annabelle, Gerry's girlfriend," as she thrust her hand out to wetly shake hands, staring squarely at Christina. Without even appearing to draw breath she pecked Gerald on the cheek and said, "I'll go and freshen up in the bedroom, it's probably not the best time to have the help in at the moment. We have so much to discuss, so much to plan for the next few weeks. I'll leave you to make our apologies. Hurry back so that we can finish our discussion." Then off she flounced with a skip to Gerald's bedroom, towing her case behind her.

Gerald hadn't changed his expression in the thirty seconds that this farcical sketch had played out, except that as the last few seconds passed he appeared to have the onset of some nervous disease as his head started to gently shake from side to side involuntarily. Christina broke the silence again, from behind Mme Joella, and in her soft tone said with a smile,

"Monsieur Gerald, I am sorry. I didn't mean to disturb you. Perhaps we can reschedule for some other time when you don't have so much to plan. Au revoir!" And with that, for the second time Mme Joella reached in and pulled the door closed whilst staring unemotionally at Gerald.

Gerald stood facing the door in the same position for a full minute his head still gently rocking from side to side. "What just happened?" he said out loud, as if expecting an answer to miraculously ring out.

He turned back into the room. He hadn't noticed Annabelle's eyes narrowing, her jawline clenching ever so slightly, as if readying for battle.

"How dare you Annabelle, just...just how dare you walk back into my life and create such wanton havoc!" It was amazing that Gerald could string together any form of sentence, as his temples throbbed and the pins and needles in his finger tips distracted him. He continued in an uncharacteristically dominant tone, such as he had never used before with Annabelle. "You dare to walk back into my life after draining me emotionally and financially, waltzing off with your *toyboy* lover leaving me in pieces. Then...then you turn up here after all this time as if nothing ever happened."

Gerald felt good now. He began to feel emancipated from something that had long festered. Annabelle's leaving had been so quick before that he hadn't had the time or, having been worn down for some time, the personal strength to tell Annabelle what he thought. This had lived with him all this time since that fateful day.

"'I don't like you Annabelle. You are not a very nice person!" he stated.

Unfortunately, Gerald almost said it sympathetically, although that was far from his intention. Annabelle seized that moment of weakness.

She had been sitting cross legged on the settee, fingers locked in her lap and listening in her, oh so condescending way that Gerald hated. She uncrossed her legs, untangled her fingers in a controlled manner and stood up right in front of Gerald, breaching his usual personal space.

"Gerry," she paused, "Gerry dear, when I met you, you were nothing, a scared little man with small dreams and no ambitions. You would never have left England and travelled here to this lovely exciting life; in fact, you would not have gone anywhere without me. You are still a scared little man—you would be nothing without my care and the way I have moulded you!"

Now, usually Annabelle knew that this subtle put-down would have quashed Gerald, but Gerald was not the Gerald of the past; he was up for the challenge now, no more submissive Gerald.

"Once again, Annabelle, you are not a nice person!" he retorted. "You moulded me okay. You moulded me into something weaker than I ever was, someone who was ashamed of his own body, someone who lost every piece of the little confidence I ever did have. I want you to leave! I want you to leave me alone, and I want you never to enter my life again."

Unflinching and with a wry smile Annabelle drove forward, raising her tone ever so slightly.

"You owe me Gerald; you owe me!"

Gerald, in some unconscious flash of genius, sidestepped Annabelle and walked to the key hooks by the kitchen door. He carefully lifted the keys to Bella off the hook, walked back to Annabelle and thrust them into her hand.

"That's all I have left Annabelle; she's parked in the square!"

Annabelle closed her manicured hand over the keys, walked to the bedroom and retrieved her wheelie case. She squeakily wheeled the case out past Gerald, without a word, without a look, and just like that she was gone, clip clopping down the stone stairs and away across the courtyard.

Gerald stood and smiled, happy with his standing and happy that he had finally bested Annabelle. His smile turned to a grimace a second later as he remembered Christina.

Chapter Twelve

A Perilous Journey For Love

As soon as he had composed himself, Gerald left his apartment and ran as fast as his gangly legs would carry him across the town to where Mme LaFoy lived and, more importantly, where Christina was staying. It had been a full forty minutes since Annabelle had departed and Gerald had so much to explain to Christina.

"She has left, Monsieur Gerald," Mme LaFoy stated, standing on her porch with a cynical smirk

Agitated that he had to ask a further question Gerald said,

"Where has she gone to, please?"

With an equally cynical and smarmy smile Mme responded in a tone a whole octave higher,

"Home to where she lives and she has friends who care about her; to Lyon of course."

Gerald bit his tongue again, which in his current state was sapping his fortitude.

"Merci Madame LaFoy," he said again with a false smile, and turned on his heel back down what had most recently been a happy path.

Mme LaFoy, doubly discontented at the way her lady friend appeared to have been treated and that the conversation with Gerald had not been more satisfyingly abrasive, shouted after him in an altogether out of character shrill tone,

"You English are all the same—too amorous!" She quickly stepped back inside and shut the door heavily, so as not to give the pig Englishman the time to respond.

Gerald paused his step, his eyes wide and his nostrils flared. His English decorum restrained him from turning around, tempting as it was to respond. He stepped off again and quickened his pace back towards his apartment, his eyes glazed with feelings of anger, sadness and fear. A single word repeated itself in his fuddled brain— *Amorous*. As he eventually walked up the narrow rue towards his apartment he stated loudly,

"I've known bloody monks that have been more amorous than me!" which caused the two elderly women sitting outside on their polished front steps to interrupt their conversation and let out a muffled snigger.

Gerald got back to his apartment. His chest was tight and his head swimming as he mulled the thought that the best woman he had ever met had been lost because of his Nemesis, Annabelle. It was definitely not the best time to make any rash decisions. Gerald then did exactly that. He grabbed his jacket, helmet and wallet from the apartment. What he proposed was not only foolhardy but dangerous. But for the first time in his life he actually believed he was in love. He pushed his fully charged bike out into the street from the courtyard of Mme Joella's house and whirred off towards the bike shop in the city. One more thing was necessary before he made the journey north—a spare battery for his ride.

Some 25 miles away from Clairville begins the arterial route north. One can either take the slower B roads which wind their way through the many towns and villages or the auto route for which a toll is due. At the toll areas the dual carriageways in each direction fan out to ten lanes to accommodate the traffic who want to pay the toll to take the faster, less crowded route north and southbound. In fact, the routes were always quiet out of holiday season due to most of the heavy haulage preferring to use the old B routes where the better Routier restaurants lie. It was about 2pm and in booth number three the young female attendant was sitting in her warm, cramped environment with the fan whirring, dozing in a half sleep. Most of the traffic was utilising the auto pay booths and she had been in the same daze all morning. As she stared in her sleepy state back down the wide, monotonous, concrete approach to the toll barriers her eyes could just make out a speck approaching. She was used to the outline of most vehicles but this was something different; she screwed her eyes up to get a better focus. Motorcycle? No too slow and she was well aware of the attributed roar to such. As the speck grew into a discernible shape she recognised the outline of a cyclist. But it was too fast for a normal bicycle and anyway everyone knew that bicycles were not allowed on the autoroutes. Before she could work out any more, the screaming hum of Gerald's ride had passed her in a blur of silver and black. Slipping through the narrow gap between the end of the barrier and the next booth Gerald waved cordially with one hand and faded into the distance, northbound on the dual carriageway. The booth attendant picked up her telephone and composed herself ready to explain to her supervisor.

Gerald was pleased he was making what he thought was good time. His original battery was still a third charged and the new spare sitting strapped to the back of his bike was fully charged. He had every confidence of reaching Lyon within the next twenty four hours. Just 2 miles north of the toll booths on a raised section of the hard shoulder, reserved for the emergency services, sat Officer Giroud in his 'Police' marked Renault Laguna estate car. His morning had also been slow, there was only so much enthusiasm he could muster for examining the driver's hours of the few heavy goods vehicles that had passed and the one *speeder* that he had ticketed. As Gerald whizzed past him, flat down on his handlebars to reduce resistance, Officer Giroud sat and puzzled to himself with a questioning look on his face—was he on the A or the B road? Having satisfied himself where he actually was he shrugged his shoulders and selected first, switching on his lights and sirens as he did so. It didn't take the officer very long to speed up the autoroute and then slow down to pull up at a crawling forty five kilometres per hour behind Gerald in a prone position on his bike. Gerald looked, and looked again in his rear view mirror, to see the myriad of flashing lights and Officer Giroud's finger indicating towards the hard shoulder. Gerald throttled off and pulled over.

Officer Giroud parked his car in a fend off position and stepped out of the vehicle. The following five minutes of conversation between the officer and Gerald could be best summarised through the visual medium of a silent movie. Each time a vehicle flew past the two men on the hard shoulder the occupant of the vehicle would get a still frame of the melodrama being played out.

Officer Giroud remonstrating with Gerald.

Gerald remonstrating with Officer Giroud.

Officer Giroud stepping back with his right hand on his holster.

Gerald standing with his hands aloft in surrender.

Officer Giroud with an outstretched 'stop' hand.

Gerald down on one knee with his hands clenched in front of him in a pleading manner.

Officer Giroud standing with both his hands up, questioning.

Gerald pointing towards the north and Officer Giroud looking north.

Gerald sobbing uncontrollably with his hands in the air again.

Officer Giroud with an outstretched 'stop' hand, again.

Gerald crying on Officer Giroud's shoulder as the officer hugged him, weeping also.

Officer Giroud, stern faced, pointing north in a Napoleonic pose.

Gerald, hands high in the air again, laughing, joyously.

Both men hugging and laughing.

By the time ten minutes had passed the electric bike had been loaded into the voluminous Laguna boot, Officer Giroud had conceded that riding the bike on the autoroute was a *Crime Passionnel* and the two men were locked on a mission for *L'Amour*. As the police car sped north, sirens blaring and lights flashing, Officer Giroud radioed his dispatcher and requested details of an address in Lyon. News soon spread to the head of the intelligence section, Detective Inspector Madeleine Corbeau, who insisted that Officer Giroud bring this lovelorn Englishman to meet her. The flying visit at the front foyer of Lyon Police Headquarters saw Gerald re-telling the whole epic saga to DI Corbeau, seven of her female administration staff and one man, Stefan from Resources, all of whom were drawing tissues from the same box at the end of Gerald's tale. Eventually DI Corbeau handed a confidential envelope to Officer Giroud and wished Gerald 'Bon Chance'. As the two left on their mission, DI Corbeau the admin' girls and Stefan had already planned the castigation of their poor, unsuspecting, unromantic menfolk.

In the envelope were three addresses for women in the greater Lyon area with the name Christina Dubois; Gerald had been unsure of any middle names to narrow the search. They decided to attack the task by heading for the closest geographically. At the first address Officer Giroud had much explanation to make when the woman who answered the door had semi-collapsed thinking that something had happened to her 18-year-old daughter, Christina, who was studying in Paris. Officer Giroud had to make several frantic telephone calls to get young Christina out of lessons and onto the telephone to her mother who was being comforted by Gerald with increasingly large shots of Cognac. When they eventually left the slightly inebriated and tearful Ms Dubois on the telephone to her bemused daughter Christina, both men drew a huge breath and sighed simultaneously.

At the next address, they decided that Gerald should make the house call with Officer Giroud in close backup. The second Christina Dubois was a forty something singleton who, in a word was vivacious, with platinum blonde locks and was wearing a tight fitting evening dress at four o'clock in the afternoon, as if she had been waiting for this moment her whole lifetime. She became very intent on getting Gerald to come inside and view her collection of porcelain unicorns, even after he had explained that she was not the Christina Dubois he had been looking for. Officer Giroud stepped up at this moment, having recognised this was not the woman Gerald was looking for and prised Gerald from Ms Dubois' strong grasp. As the two men left the disappointed Ms Dubois, Officer Giroud handed her his business card should she require any further assistance at a later date, which seemed to go some way to placating the insistent woman.

The final address was on the affluent outskirts of the city and as they drove there Gerald stated to his new friend that he was sure this would be the one. They finally drew up outside the tall, immaculate town house with the neatly manicured front garden and Gerald was doubly sure this was his Christina's home. Only one thing turned his positive feelings to sadness. The large fresh looking 'To Let' sign which sat squarely in the front garden hanging over the footpath and the obviously empty rooms on the ground floor. Gerald and Officer Giroud sat for a full thirty seconds with the engine running and staring at the sign. Officer Giroud was the first to break the trance and grasped Gerald's forearm and said, 'Fortitude my friend, fortitude'.

He alighted from the police car and began enquiries. After about forty minutes, which seemed to Gerald like hours, he returned. Officer Giroud sat in the car and stated, that from the description, it did, in fact, seem as if this was where Gerald's Christina lived. The neighbours, who were new to the street, only knew that the pleasant woman had returned briefly, in the last day or so, and a large removal van had taken all her belongings within a day of her return and they had not seen her since. Officer Giroud even contacted the selling agent but they wouldn't release any details without a written request from the police for fear of breaching any data protection laws.

Gerald said nothing all the way to Lyon's central rail station. He and Officer Giroud unstrapped and unloaded the cycle from the rear of the car. Gerald hugged Officer Giroud as his brother, trying to explain how indebted he was to the officer, who just held up a quieting hand. Gerald then wheeled the bike onto the carriage and the train pulled away from the platform heading south for Marseille and home.

The following day Gerald felt jaded from the previous day's exploits and a lack of sleep, thinking of Christina and what could have been. He had not felt so low for as long as he could remember. He wandered the town for the morning looking at stuff that he never knew he needed in the hardware store, sipping coffee for hours at Le Petit Lemon until it was too cold to drink. Hugo, although he had tried, was unable to console his friend and in the end thought it best just to leave Gerald to his thoughts. Gerald fixed his stare out of the bar window to the side street. He did not even perceive the bar's front door opening.

"Monsieur Gerald, there you are!" Christina's voice startled Gerald. He stood quickly and in the process jolted the table and his cold cup of coffee, spilling some on the table. Gerald fumbled with the cup to prevent any further catastrophe. He pulled the chair from behind him and in a very un-Gerald like moment gently hugged Christina with the total joy at seeing her. Realising, he apologised to Christina, but she just smiled and held up her hand to stop him.

"Please have a seat with me," Gerald finally managed to say. They both sat at the small round table and Gerald ordered two more coffees from Hugo for them.

"I've missed you," said Gerald, then again not wanting to be too forward, "I mean I've missed you about the town."

Christina knew what Gerald meant. She explained,

"I had to return to Lyon to settle some business matters."

"Oh!" said Gerald, not wanting to divulge that he knew exactly that. They both sipped their creamy coffees.

"But now you will be seeing me here much more, as I am in the process of trying to buy a property."

"Oh good," said Gerald, gaining a smile from Christina.

She continued, "Gerald, I think you are a wonderful man, and I've enjoyed your company so much. You are one of the first men that I can honestly say I feel comfortable with after the loss of my dear husband. but..." she paused.

Gerald's heart sank - had he been wrong? He felt as if he was getting the 'easy let down' of which he had been so used to in the past. Christina went on trying to find the correct words.

"I enjoy our time with each other and I don't want that to change, Gerald, but at this time I have to spend some more of the time with Phillipe. I have some very difficult decisions to make about my life in the next few months. I do hope you understand?"

Gerald's sickly grin did not give away the pressure of the blood and adrenalin coursing through his head and body at that time. In his head he just kept hearing the same thing—Renoir! Renoir! Gerald pulled himself together and managed to blurt,

"Of course, of course. It will be lovely if we can still see each other now and then. Anyway I have to apologise; I have to go and attend to a thing. I hope you don't mind?" He stood up and took Christina's hand and shook it.

Christina managed to say,

"Oh! Of course Gerald, maybe I can call on you tomorrow?"

Gerald was already at the front door, as he called back,

"Yes, that would be good. Cheerio!" And he was gone across the square. Christina turned back to her coffee with a slightly puzzled face which the ever present Hugo had noticed. As if perceiving Hugo's glance, she looked across to him. Hugo looked back and shrugged his shoulders and said,

"Englishmen, eh!"

Chapter Thirteen

Mano-a-mano

The following morning, Gerald woke and lay very still in bed. Every sinew, muscle and joint ached from his earlier travels. He used waiting for Henri's alarm fart as an excuse just to stay reclined and not in pain. Then he remembered what his task was for the day and he rolled and gingerly ascended from his bed and headed for the shower. Gerald double scrubbed every orifice and crack, and stepping from the hot shower used his towel like a yoga implement to try to loosen his stiff and unresponsive body. He wrapped the towel around his waist, walked into the kitchen and poured a strong black coffee from the bubbling pot, and set to dressing himself. He pulled out his best suit, a beige linen two piece he'd obtained in a Debenham's sale back in the UK, years earlier. To his credit it still fitted over the blue silky shirt he chose to wear. Standing in front of his full length dress mirror he slipped on his suede loafers and looked at himself. He licked his finger and smoothed his eyebrows to match his freshly brushed hair. He then sprayed himself liberally with what was left of his Eau Sauvage and surveyed himself again in the mirror. He was satisfied that he would pass muster; after all, he knew that he was going to be facing his fashion Nemesis, Phillipe Renoir.

Gerald walked to Le Petit Lemon and on entering he asked a bleary eyed Hugo for a coffee. There was no other conversation. Hugo was still slightly hung over from the day before and couldn't even be bothered to ask why Gerald was up so early and looking like he was going to a wedding. Gerald seized his coffee and took up position in the window of the bar which had a clear view of the square and the front of Phillipe Renoir's immobilier shop. At 8:55am precisely the familiar and well known, beautiful, gold coloured Citroen SM pulled in to the parking bay outside the estate agency and Phillipe Renoir got out and walked to the front door, fiddled with his keys, opened the door to the shop and walked in. Gerald's pulse rose as he watched. He didn't even know what he was going to say. He finished his third coffee and composed himself. He walked out of the bar with a cursory nod to Hugo, who didn't even acknowledge him. Hugo did, however, watch as Gerald navigated the cobbled square and over to Renoir's immobilier. Behind his puzzled look, Hugo's fuddled brain wasn't sure if it even wanted to work out what was going on.

Gerald walked up to the front door of the immobilier. It must have been his heightened sense of consciousness from the adrenaline coursing through his body that made him notice the front of the shop in detail for the first time. The facade, compared to most other shop fronts in the town, was perfect. Every painted surface was smooth as glass. Everything was clean of road dust. The brass fittings on the heavy glazed door were polished and unmarked. The properties in the window display were perfectly and evenly laid out; not a board out of place. Gerald paused before the door and straightened his jacket and re-tucked his shirt in. He pulled the cuff down on his suit and took hold of the door handle, not wanting to spoil its flawless lustre. He opened the door and walked in. The tiny bell above the inside of the door tinkled as he did so.

Inside the shop, there was no sign of Renoir. Gerald, again, noticed, unlike any time before, the interior environment. Of course he had been into the shop before but then he had been diverted with other thoughts. The open plan room, which had obviously been two rooms in the past from the exposed and aged timber stud frame to one side; the timbers now painted a cream colour his bony torso. The plastered walls exposed between the old stud frameworks around the rooms were also crisply painted with a cream paint. A large mahogany desk dominated the rear of the shop in the centre with a large, silver Apple computer taking up the left hand side of it. On the right was an Art Deco chrome stand with a naked male dancer stretching his muscular frame up to the sky. A black Mont Blanc fountain pen rested on the chrome base and a large leather blotter pad sat between the computer and the figurine. In a glass vessel, a lime coloured candle smouldered, releasing a citrus fragrance that lightly permeated the air in the large room. Behind the desk a large, winged, green leather Chesterfield chair sat at a jaunty angle on its mahogany frame and multi-wheeled base. The floor in the centre of the room was adorned with a very colourful, but not gaudy, oriental rug. To the right of the rug sat a staunch, two seat, green Chesterfield settee which gleamed in its uncreased leather skin. Like a periphery around the rest of the room were small occasional tables and shelves adorned with varying gilded, ornate silver frames from differing architectural periods, each housing a photo and details of the different properties that the agency was advertising for sale It was as if they were actually members of Phillipe Renoir's family.

Gerald stood and noticed how calm the whole room made him feel. He didn't notice Phillipe enter the room quietly from a curtained doorway on the right. Phillipe stood and watched Gerald for a full five seconds, measuring his attempt at looking chic, before Gerald noticed his rival with a start.

"Monsieur Gerald, I didn't mean to startle you. Please excuse me!" Phillipe said.

He was perfectly groomed and dressed immaculately as always; his taupe silk shirt and blue and gold Hermes tie sat under his perfectly tailored, navy Yves Saint Laurent suit, the midnight coloured material only broken by the flash of colour from the Hermes handkerchief just poking from his left breast pocket. This ensemble was complimented by his, amusingly casual, light green, English suede, brogue shoes. He walked slowly over to Gerald and stood before him. Phillipe was just slightly shorter than Gerald's six foot two inch frame.

"How may I be of service?" Phillipe said in his perfectly accented English tongue. The citrus infusion in the air couldn't mask Phillipe's subtle lemony cologne that smelled like fresh pine forests in summer. Gerald had not been able to answer and had an uncomfortable smile on his face. Phillipe focussed his gleaming tortoiseshell glasses and noticed where Gerald had missed some stubble on his neck and a left-over croissant crumb on his top lip. Above the smell of his own cologne he discerned Gerald's passable Eau Sauvage. Gerald suddenly clicked and in order to feel more comfortable moved left and walked to where one of the frame covered tables stood.

He turned to face the smiling Phillipe, brimming with confidence of what had to be said and done Gerald spoke.

"Monsieur Renoir," he began, "I have come to see you because I have been troubled by your behaviour with Madame Dubois. You may or may not know, but I have been squiring Madame Dubois for the past month and my intentions are honourable and I wish to progress our relationship to the next level." Gerald was in full flow but paused briefly before he made his next comment, which he felt uncomfortable with; he continued, "you are a handsome man, Monsieur Renoir, and I understand you have many qualities and prospects that would appeal to any woman." Gerald had dropped his head in this uncomfortable moment and did not notice a wry, almost indiscernible smile on Phillipe Renoir's face. Gerald continued again. "I have little prospects compared to a successful businessman such as yourself but I truly believe I can make Madame Dubois happy and we could learn to love each other." Gerald had run over this statement a hundred times in his head and each time he had felt more and more awkward, embarrassed and agonised over whether it sounded honest. He lifted his gaze to the face of Phillipe Renoir, as if he was waiting for the sanction of a school headmaster.

In these few short moments, Phillipe's brain had whirled and his insides quivered at this bewildering man who would confront another man for the sake of love. However, none of these emotions showed on the calm exterior of Phillipe, but an idea of such delicious proportions had evolved in his head. He moved to break the stillness between the two of them and strode as manfully as he dared to the back of his desk and lowered himself into his large leather chair. In a Bond *villainesque* manner he stroked his smoothly shaved chin and swivelled the seat of his heavy leather chair to face Gerald.

"So Monsieur Gerald, you say you love this woman?" The question was rhetorical and before Gerald could answer Phillipe went on, "Then I suggest a contest. A duel, a duel for the love of such a wonderful woman!" He raised an eyebrow in an overly theatrical way which he immediately regretted. Gerald was lost in the moment; the thought of a duel for the love of a woman, as preposterous as that may seem to someone in the modern age, actually seemed the only way to Gerald. He noticed the raised eyebrow and Phillipe's sanctimonious posture in the oversize chair and this only entrenched his thoughts—Cad! Bounder! Gerald spoke.

"Monsieur Renoir, I accept your challenge. Name the time and the place and I will fight for the right to escort Madame Dubois. But know this, I believe I love this woman and I will fight to the end to win her!"

Phillipe took a split second to savour the moment and responded,

"Very well Monsieur the place is Le Lac du sport, and my challenge to you is natation."

Gerald was lost for a second which Phillipe could see. He raised both eyebrows sighed and said

"Swimming, monsieur, swimming. If you beat me to the pontoons and back at the Lac du sport you are free to court Madame Dubois unmolested."

A quizzical look overtook Gerald; he could not have helped that look if he'd tried. He didn't want to turn this confrontation into a comedy sketch because he was more than serious about the whole matter. He would win, or drown and die a mortified man.

"Very well, Monsieur Renoir" he retorted, "swimming it is. One week from today, I will meet you at the Lac du sport. Bring a second, monsieur, to ensure fair play!" Where Gerald got the last part of his statement from he didn't know. He turned and marched from the estate agency, satisfied that he had done his best in his quest to win the woman he believed he was in love with. Phillipe Renoir sat in his enveloping leather chair and smiled to himself. Things were going well. But deep down there was a twinge of disquiet twanging at his gut.

A week to the day, Hugo waited solemnly in the square in his Citroen Pallas for Gerald to arrive. Gerald opened the passenger door and slid in to the voluminous cabin of the old car. Hugo could not contain a smile. Gerald was wearing a blue swimming hat, that appeared a little too tight with one of his ears trying to escape the confines of the tight latex dome. He carried a towel and wore a large quilted sports coat that came to his knees. As usual with Gerald he had researched the best attire for open water swimming and had purchased accordingly. The duo set off in a cloud of diesel smoke. The journey was only four miles and was traversed in silence.

After Gerald's meeting with Phillipe in the estate agent's shop, Gerald had gone straight to Le Petit Lemon and explained the situation to Hugo. After the explanation Hugo had tried to talk Gerald out of this folly but Gerald had remained staunch in his decision to carry the challenge through.

Unbeknown to Gerald and Hugo, Phillipe Renoir, over the years he had been a resident, had secured a network of women friends in the town. They listened to his problems and relationship matters and confided in him with their deepest secrets. He, to them, was a man that they would dearly love to love, but because he was such a good friend to them they knew that any carnal relationship would sour what they craved most—gossip and knowledge; in fact Phillipe Renoir had never courted such a relationship but most of the individual women who visited him never knew this. Most days that Phillipe's agency was open, local resident women would enter the shop to converse for hours and drink the sweet teas that Phillipe would brew for them. Obviously, due to the location of the agency, opposite Le Petit Lemon, Phillipe Renoir had, of course, gained some notoriety as a bit of a ladies man. The result of all this was that Phillipe was aware that Hugo was going to second for Gerald at the duel.

Le lac du sport is set in a small, pine and deciduous tree covered valley just to the south west of the town. Owned by one of the older farming families; they had diversified and opened the 30 acre lake for public use some ten years ago. It proffered a small sandy beach which had been imported by the family, camping and parking areas and a small seasonal cafe in a log cabin. Stony paths navigate the scented pine woods surrounding the perimeter of the lake, which allow peaceful rambles. The lake is predominantly used by the local community all year and the sign, indicating its existence, on the main A road is regularly pilfered by locals for a reason—to keep tourists away.

On the morning in question, Gerald and Hugo arrived at the lake in Hugo's car, which rivalled him in stature. They parked and the hydraulic suspension hissed and lowered the automobile in place like some landing spaceship. Hugo exited the driver's door in his tight, best Sunday suit, befitting of the occasion. Gerald got out of the passenger side. His blue latex swim hat gleamed in the dim, early sunlight, like the dome of some Turkish mosque at dawn. He had a large striped beach towel wrapped around his bony torso under a coat and a pair of orange Bermuda shorts which matched his worn Havaianas flip flops. Both men strode down to the pier at the edge of the pseudo beach and waited in silence. A wispy mist hung over the intimidating lake and only the echoing sound of a lonesome jackdaw rippled across Le Lac du sport. The silence was broken by the creaking sound of the ill-fitting door of the cafe lodge opening. Phillipe Renoir strode out onto the surrounding covered deck of the cafe. He wore his, bespoke, fitted, one piece neoprene suit which enhanced his understated muscular frame. He walked barefoot down to the two awaiting men by the pier. Gerald saw him approach and noticed the crest of a fiery bird emblazoned on the left chest with the motto 'per adversa ad astra' which Gerald did not know meant 'through adversity to the stars'. Phillipe Renoir, unbeknown to Gerald, was the current veteran champion at the nearby Heriot Triathlon club. As always Gerald felt that he had little to offer in this battle for the anticipated love of his life, but even so he would give his all.

Phillipe strode up to Gerald and Hugo took his designated place just behind Gerald, who fixed his stare at Phillipe and spoke in the early chill, the smoky hue from his breath swirled around his head.

"Where is your second, Monsieur?" he said,

With as much sincerity as he could muster Phillipe Renoir responded,

"Making me a warm chocolat in the café, monsieur. Shall we get on with the challenge?"

"Yes, yes!" a clearly flustered Gerald responded.

Hugo stood behind Gerald with an emotionless stern face and the hint of a knowledgeable smile. He stepped forward and ceremoniously took Gerald's towel with two pinched hands, flapping the large towel back with a crack, like a matador with a cloak, and folded it over his arm.

Gerald began star jumping and limbering up his white, wiry body. In an attempt to make Gerald feel comfortable and in a strangely empathic move Phillipe began stretching and swinging his arms. Hugo broke the exercise regime between the two men, conscious that Le Petit Lemon opened in two hours.

"Messieurs, shall we begin?" he stated, rather than questioned, in a solemn manner befitting the occasion.

Gerald and Phillipe nodded and began their short walk to the end of the small timber pier that led to where the lake was of sufficient depth to dive off it; Hugo marched just behind them. In the centre of the lake, a mere one hundred and fifty metres away, languished the square, timber, sunbathing pontoon. Both men took up a position at the end of the pier. Phillipe turned his head to Gerald and said,

"It is not too late to cease this foolishness, Monsieur Gerald." Gerald stared ahead and responded,

"Monsieur Renoir, thank you for your concern but this is something I have to do. I love the woman that you seem keen to philander with and to that end I must do this to protect her."

Phillipe Renoir saw no further cause to pursue the conversation and nodded to Hugo. Hugo cleared his throat and both men took up position ready to dive in to the murky waters.

"Gentlemen, take your marks, on the count of three you will begin," Hugo stated and then continued, "Une, deux...trois!"

Gerald launched himself forward, eyes shut, breath held, his outstretched arms pointed to break the water's surface, his gangly following legs flailing apart slightly, his swim hat pushed up onto his head a little to expose his large ears. He hit the water in a perfect belly flop, causing a slapping sound that could be heard at the other end of the lake. Gerald kept his face in the cold water; he didn't notice the raw stinging pain on his chest and thighs. He held his breath and began kicking with his legs and windmilling his arms as quickly as he was able. Phillipe Renoir had not moved; he watched his opponent's flat dive and exuberant stroke with some admiration. He flexed into a perfect pike form, bent his knees and launched himself off the pier, hitting the surface of the water at a near perfect forty five degree angle, the surface tension of the water hardly rippling as he entered.

Gerald had made progress of some fifteen metres as Phillipe entered the water behind him. At that point Gerald lifted his face from the carpy tasting waters to draw his first breath into his burning lungs. As he did so his lateral vision perceived his opponent who, surprisingly to Gerald, seemed to be behind him. Phillipe surfaced some five metres behind him, breaking in to a nonchalant looking stroke and breathing pattern to both sides, his legs hardly moving and only a third of his head breaching the surface; the classic stoke of a seasoned distance swimmer. Gerald noticed none of this as he drew a large breath and drove his four limbs as powerfully as he could to propel him through the water.

Gerald laboured on towards the pontoon. Phillipe could see Gerald and wasn't inclined to destroy his valiant opponent and so tempered his stroke to keep an even distance behind him. As Gerald approached the floating timber structure he noticed Phillipe still behind him. This glimpse spurred him on, he touched the pontoon with a flat hand and found a foothold on the slimy timbers and pushed himself off as hard as he could toward the distant shore. Phillipe cruised in some fifteen seconds later; not breaking stroke he executed a consummate tumble turn, thrusting off from the timber shuttering on the sides of the pontoon he slid under the surface, his elongated frame torpedoed past his opponent's thrashing form by some five metres; breaking the surface slightly he instigated an up tempo stroke and glided away from the hapless and none the wiser Gerald.

Gerald continued his laboured stroke towards shore, breathing as and when he had to. His body was confused as to where to deploy his oxygen reserves—his inflamed limbs or his pounding brain. The fishy waters seemed to be able to enter his mouth, nose and ears with ease, dribbling into his airways, but he had no time to clear it or cough or deal with the ensuing panic that he was in fact drowning. He persevered and within minutes he began to touch the slimy sands at the edge of the lake. He reached a point where he couldn't perform a stroke with his arms. He quickly lowered his legs and felt his knees ground out on the soft bottom. He pushed with his arms and raised himself onto his feet but the resistance of the water impeded his wish to start running for the shore and he twisted and sat backwards rather than falling face forward in to the water. This gave him his first chance to see where his opponent was behind him. He looked and all he surveyed was his own foaming wake leading to the shore. Gerald' s heart sank. He twisted around and saw Hugo walking to the water's edge with his striped swim towel. Behind Hugo he saw the lithe frame of Phillipe Renoir with a towel around his shoulders sipping a steaming mug of hot chocolate surrounded by a gaggle of his female confidants. Gerald's head drooped and he turned to stare back at the lake in despair.

"Gerald, come!" he heard Hugo calling. He raised himself from the lapping water and trudged to where Hugo waited with his towel. His friend wrapped it around his shoulders and spoke softly. "All will be well, Gerald. You did your best, my friend."

Gerald walked with as much stature as he could to where Phillipe stood warming his hands and face from the hot mug and beverage. Gerald stopped in front of him and looked straight in to Phillipe's large, deep brown eyes.

"Monsieur Renoir, it appears you have beaten me fairly and squarely, by some distance. I have to concede you are a better man than me in this challenge that I accepted. I shall step aside and will do nothing to impede you and Madame Christina in your relationship. But know this, should any emotional harm come to Madame Christina, I shall hold you personally responsible. She is a wonderful woman and deserves only the best of life."

Phillipe Renoir nodded solemnly to Gerald and then handed his mug of chocolate to one of the attentive ladies in waiting. Phillipe stepped forward and placed his hands on Gerald's towel draped shoulders, his own towel dropping to ground as he did so. "Monsieur Gerald, you are a brave and worthy challenger for any man for the hand of a woman." Phillipe then leaned in slowly and placed a kiss on each of Gerald's cheeks. Phillipe drew back only slightly, looked into Gerald's eyes and then slowly he kissed Gerald fully on the mouth for a full three seconds. Both men tasted the pond like flavour of each other, although Gerald could still smell the lemony aroma of Phillipe's after shave. Gerald was frozen to the sandy spot. Phillipe drew back and then leaned in close to Gerald's left ear, away from the admiring looks and ears of the gathered women and Hugo. Phillipe spoke softly to Gerald.

"Monsieur Gerald, I dearly love Madame Christina, but not in the way you love her. I have more feelings for you, you crazy, wonderful Englishman. Gerald, I am gay and I am deeply jealous of my good friend, Christina, and the fact that she has the endearing feelings of passion from a man such as you."

Phillipe, brushed Gerald cheek to cheek and pecked him one more time on the lips, before he released his hands from Gerald's shoulders, collected his towel from the ground, retrieved his still steaming chocolate from the women and walked off towards the cafe.

Gerald's simple brain was whirring and trying to analyse what had just occurred. Apart from the fact that he had never been kissed so passionately before he was reeling from what Phillipe Renoir had said. Phillipe's entourage broke to follow him up to the café. As they thinned out Gerald saw Christina standing at the back of the crowd, where she had been waiting with a steaming cup of chocolate for both Phillipe and Gerald since Gerald had begun his return journey back from the pontoon. She walked to where Gerald was still rooted to the spot and put the hot chocolate into his cold hands to warm him. She tilted her head to one side slightly and smiled, in one of the unconscious mannerisms that Gerald so loved, as she spoke in a slightly mocking way,

"So my lovely Gerald, it appears that you lost the competition for my affections?".

Gerald's forehead frowned slightly and his eyes dropped from hers.

"Yes…" he said in a lowered tone still unsure of what was fact or fantasy at that moment.

"Well", she said in a hushed tone, "Why don't we go back to your apartment and discuss where we go from here?"

"Yes, yes of course," Gerald said, looking back into her eyes and at last making some reality of the whole situation.

After the short drive from the lake to town in Christina's car, the pair ascended to Gerald's quiet apartment. Gerald insisted that he take a shower before they talk about anything, so he furnished Christina with a chilled glass of rosé wine and hurried off for a speedy but necessary shower. He emerged back into the lounge some five minutes later in his large dressing gown fluffing his hair with a clean towel. As he did so there was no sign of Christina. His heart sank slightly until he heard her soft voice coming from Gerald's bedroom. "In here my darling"

Gerald walked to the bedroom door, a quizzical look on his face. He pushed the plank door open with the back of his hand whilst holding his own glass of wine. The large plantation blinds were pushed closed, the bedside lights were glowing and Christina sat in Gerald's bed with her knees drawn up and the throw pulled up under her arms revealing naked shoulders. Gerald deduced that the rest of Christina's body was in a similar state of undress.

"Come and get in the warm with me." she invited.

Gerald, in a habitual move, conditioned into him by Annabelle, switched the lights off at the switch by the door, but Christina shook her head and said, "Gerald, please leave the lights on, I want to be able to look at you when I make love to you." Gerald smiled slightly, switched the lights back on and moved to the edge of the bed, where in another self-conscious habit he disrobed himself facing away from Christina and slid back into the bed between the sheets and gently into Christina's warm embrace.

Later that afternoon the silky sound of Brook Benton mixed with the smell of onions sautéing in butter wafted from Gerald's balcony doors. Inside the apartment Gerald and Christina stood at the cooking counter, she slicing aubergines, Gerald gently cooking the onions for the ratatouille and watching the butter sizzling. Both were totally naked apart from a cotton apron that each wore to stop any accidents with the spitting butter. Their buttocks moved in unison together to the rhythm of the music. Gerald watched the hot pan slowly browning the onions and listened to Christina humming to the music beside him.

At that moment Gerald knew that he was the happiest he had ever been in his whole miserable life and he vowed to himself that he was going to spend the rest of his life focussed on ensuring this wonderful woman was always as happy as he felt right then. Gerald leaned across and tenderly kissed the smiling Christina on her soft cheek.

The End